Secret Lies

When her mother, Laureen, elopes, thirteen-year-old Elvira Judson is forced to go to Charlottesville, Virginia, to stay with distant relatives. Proud, lonely, and hurt, she turns to fantasy for solace; her dreams, as always, center on the father she has never met. In Elvira's mind he is distinguished, loving, and rich—all the things her mother is not. Aunt Carrie and Cousin Henry do their kindly best, but Elvira's conviction grows; any day now her father will appear to carry her off to the life she deserves. But an unforeseen meeting with her father's sister shatters Elvira's hopes and threatens to undermine her sense of self.

Sensitively drawn, *Secret Lies* is a convincing portrayal of a young girl's struggle to surrender her fantasies in order to realize the love and acceptance she has always longed for.

Secret Lies

BY SARAH SARGENT

Crown Publishers, Inc.

NEW YORK

Manufactured in the United States of America
Published simultaneously in Canada by General Publishing Company Limited
10   9   8   7   6   5   4   3   2   1

The text of this book is set in 11 pt. Caledonia.

Library of Congress Cataloging in Publication Data
Sargent, Sarah.
Secret lies.
Summary: Thirteen-year-old Elvira arrives at her
aunt's home in the hills of Virginia full of fantasies
about the father she has never known and her mother's
prejudices about life in a small town.
[1. Family life — Fiction.   2. Mothers and daughters
— Fiction.   3. Virginia — Fiction]   I. Title.
PZ7.S2479Se   1981   [Fic]   81-7799
ISBN 0-517-54291-9   AACR2

For my aunts, the DuPuy sisters:
Josephine
Florine
Alice
Katherine
Anne
A remarkable group of Virginia ladies

Secret Lies

1

NEVER AGAIN was she going to cry. Never, Elvira swore to herself, standing in the principal's office at nine-thirty on Monday morning, her eyes still puffy from the night before. If she hadn't been so tired from crying and hadn't forgotten to set the alarm, she wouldn't have been an hour late for school, and nobody would have been poking around, asking for a note from her mother explaining why she was late.

"She's out of town," Elvira told the secretary.

"Out of town?" The secretary raised her eyebrows. "And who is staying with you?"

"You can't stay by yourself," Mr. Hurlburt, the principal, told her when the secretary rushed her into his office. "Aside from everything else, it's just illegal. A thirteen-year-old can't do that. Where exactly is your mother?" Not half-listening to her, he reached for the phone to call Mrs. Macy, the school social worker, a cube-shaped lady with a voice like a frog. Elvira

1

had never expected to be forced to explain her private life to a social worker. Elvira was quiet in school. She liked to think she kept a mysterious air about her, so that people would guess she was somehow special.

But never mind what Elvira felt. Mrs. Macy came after school Monday afternoon and plopped herself down on Elvira's sofa. She opened up her notebook and smiled, trying to act friendly. How could somebody be your friend and make you into a case in a notebook at the same time? Elvira wondered. Mopping off her nose one minute and picking at invisible fuzz on her skirt the next, Mrs. Macy got set to write up Elvira's case. When she leaned forward, Elvira saw breasts as pale as fish bellies floating around loose. Elvira felt sick.

"Now, dear, where has your mother gone? What arrangements has she made for you?"

"She's only on a short trip," Elvira lied. Actually, Laureen hadn't said how long she'd be gone. The note left all that for Elvira to figure out. Unfortunately, Elvira was good at reading between the lines. Her mother had run off with Duane to get married. That was what had happened. She wanted Elvira to move out—that's what she really meant.

"My mother is on a wedding trip, that's all," Elvira explained. "She got married over the weekend. They won't be gone long. She has to go back to work and all. So will Duane."

"Duane? Oh, that's the man she married? Do you know him well, Elvira?"

"Sure," Elvira said, her voice sharp. "Of course I know him. My mother wouldn't go off and marry some stranger, would she?"

"I'm sure it's all a shock to you, dear," Mrs. Macy said sooth-

2

ingly. "I just want to help you. What do you feel your mother would like you to do, just until she comes back? Did she make any plans for you?"

"If I want to, she said I could go and stay with her aunt in Charlottesville, Virginia," Elvira said. "But I don't need to do that except in an emergency or something. She expects me to stay here and take care of the apartment and all." That was a lie. Laureen was shipping her off, all right.

Sunday night—*last* night. It seemed a month ago, Elvira realized, startled. Last night, about eight o'clock, Elvira had come home from the sleep-over at Jennifer Weber's. There had been that note, stuck up on the refrigerator door. Elvira knew Laureen was spending the weekend with Duane. In the three months her mother had been going with him, Elvira had seen it getting more and more serious. She hadn't admitted it to herself, but she had been afraid something like this would happen. So before she read it, she almost knew what the note would say.

> *Precious,*
> *Surprise! Surprise! You're*
> *going to have a daddy. Duane and*
> *I just upped and tied the knot. I*
> *wanted my little girl there, but you*
> *know how Duane is when his mind is*
> *made up. Precious, you take the money*
> *under the sugar bowl and go stay with*
> *Aunt Carrie until we get back and*
> *settled. That way you'll get to have*
> *a trip too. Right, hon? Hold good*
> *thoughts, Elvira. See you soon, lamb.*
> > *Love always,*
> > *Laureen*

3

Sneaking off in that rusty bucket of Duane's on Saturday, the minute her back was turned. "Hold good thoughts!" That came straight off that evangelist program Laureen watched on TV.

"Isn't he cute, Elvira?" Laureen had said once, looking glassy-eyed at the evangelist in his suit and tie. "Don't you love those manly eyebrows? I always had a weakness for bushy-browed men."

Duane had big, bushy brows, too, come to think of it. Hair all over him like some ape. Elvira clenched her teeth in rage. Of course, her mother should get married again. It wasn't that. Elvira wasn't one to stand in the way of somebody's happiness. But not to Duane. Not after having been married to her father.

Laureen never would say much about Elvira's father, just a hint here and there. He had left when Elvira was a baby. Was Laureen to blame somehow? Had she hurt him deeply so he could never come back? Elvira had read books where that sort of thing happened.

From the first night Duane had come over—wrists sticking out of his turned-back sleeves, chains dangling around his neck—Elvira had gotten an icy feeling in her stomach. Laureen bubbled around him, all lilac lipstick and gardenia water. Little pats, laughing all the time, as if all of a sudden everything were funny. Forgetting all about having a daughter, it seemed to Elvira. "She'll get over it," Elvira remembered telling her best friend, Jennifer Weber, the night Laureen had gone off and forgotten to leave money for their pizza. One of about fifty promises she had forgotten all about as soon as Duane had come into her life. "Laureen won't be going out with him long," Elvira had said to Jennifer. "It's just a phase she's going through."

4

Elvira had tried her best to get her mother to see reason. "Laureen, don't you think those shoes might be a mistake? In those heels, you'll be looking right down onto Duane's bald spot." Laureen had always claimed to hate short men.

But her mother was past listening to common sense. Once last winter, Elvira remembered now, Laureen had stood in the doorway, watching Mrs. Axtehelm from across the hall teetering toward the elevator in her platform shoes, bracelets and rings jingling. Eyes wide, Laureen had turned to Elvira. "That's me. Twenty more years, Elvira, and that's your mother."

At the time, Elvira had crossed that off as her mother's way. Laureen liked to be dramatic. But now she put that moment together with others: the way Laureen had been painting her nails purple, waving her hands in the air like birds to dry the polish. Tweezing and spraying and curling and oiling herself for an hour before she got into her waitress uniform and went off to work. Lately she'd been staring into the mirror, leaning into the lights, pushing up the skin around her eyes, asking Elvira if she had seen any little crow's-feet, any little trenches next to her mouth.

Laureen must have figured it was Duane now or nothing later. Just took him and ran. Stuck that note on the refrigerator with the lavender tape she used to flatten her face curls at night. Just hightailed off without a second thought, leaving Elvira to sit in the living room with a caseworker and explain why her own mother hadn't bothered to tell her she was getting married.

"I'm sure she just meant me to use the money for a ticket in an emergency or something," Elvira said again. "I can stay here and wait for them to get back. I'm sure that's what she really meant." Elvira sat up straight and tried to look proud. Some

5

people probably did say she was stuck-up, but she didn't care. Elvira *was* smarter than most of them. She was headed for better things. Even if Laureen was just a waitress and they were living a little poor now. It was temporary, until the permanent part of her life started. She and Jennifer Weber spent hours talking about the future. Jennifer was going to be a ballet dancer and Elvira was going to be a novelist. Both of them were going to live in New York.

Mrs. Macy sighed. "I know you are a capable girl, Elvira. We all know that. I talked to Mr. Johnson and he said you are doing straight-A work, in fact. That's wonderful, dear. There are only three weeks left, and there won't be a problem with your passing into eighth grade next year, wherever you are. You don't have to worry about that." She reached over and patted Elvira's knee.

"I can take care of myself," Elvira said, scrunching into her chair so that nothing showed but her legs from the knees down and her big dark eyes. Black hair covered her shoulders like a tent.

Mrs. Macy cleared her throat. "It's not safe, dear," she said. "And, beyond that, it's illegal. Against the law. We have to find you a nice place to stay, Elvira, just until your mother has had time to straighten things out. A little trip, visit your mother's aunt, what's so wrong with that? Many of us would love to take a few weeks off and have a nice trip to Virginia. I'm sure I would."

She was starting to look impatient. Mrs. Macy probably had a list of problem homes to visit this afternoon. Elvira had heard Mr. Johnson use that phrase talking to the principal in the hall. "So and so comes from a problem home environment," he'd said

6

in that official tone teachers used when they talked about some kid whose mother got drunk all the time or who was bounced from one foster home to another like Jimmy Copeland.

Now Elvira was one of those.

"Do you know your aunt, dear?" Mrs. Macy asked. "When did you see her?"

"Never." Elvira was not going to give an inch.

"Really?" Mrs. Macy sounded surprised. "But she's your closest relative!"

"Not since I was two." Otherwise, Mrs. Macy would think her whole family was in the habit of deserting each other. "Laureen and I lived in Virginia until then. We stayed with Aunt Carrie for a year. But I don't remember her."

"Hasn't she kept up with you, dear? Written?" Elvira could see that Mrs. Macy was trying to get some idea how dependable this other home was, to decide if Elvira would be going off to somebody even more shiftless than Laureen. Actually, Laureen's Aunt Carrie was very dependable. She was the only person who always remembered Elvira's birthday. Laureen forgot it half the time. Aunt Carrie always sent a card and some kind of present, an out-of-style sweater or knee sox.

"She writes. At Christmas and stuff," Elvira admitted. "I'm sure, in an emergency, she would be glad to have me. But she's pretty old. She retired last year. And besides that, my mother said she has a *really* old man living with her. A distant cousin that she took in because he was too feeble to take care of himself."

"She sounds very responsible and kind," Mrs. Macy said. "What did she do before she retired, Elvira?"

"A nurse," Elvira said. "She used to be a nurse."

7

Mrs. Macy smiled. "Well, Elvira, it looks as if everything will work out fine. Just give me your aunt's address and phone number, and let me call her this afternoon. If it suits her, I'll go ahead and make your train reservations. Your mother left money for a ticket?"

Elvira nodded. She felt cornered, on the edge of tears. But she clenched her teeth. No one—not Mrs. Macy, or even Jennifer— would find out how she felt. Elvira got up and looked in the end table drawer. She flipped through Laureen's address book until she got to her Aunt Carrie. She handed it to Mrs. Macy, with her finger in the right place.

"Thank you, dear," Mrs. Macy said, jerking her frizzy head up like a lizard. "I'll call and have a chat with your Aunt Carrie. Don't worry about a thing." She smiled at Elvira. "I know you are very grown-up for a thirteen-year-old, Elvira, and I think we can bend the rules in your case. I spoke to Mrs. Axtehelm across the hall, and she agreed to watch out for you tonight. So you can stay here as usual. By tomorrow, we'll have more permanent arrangements made."

Elvira didn't want to go off to Charlottesville and live in the woods. She wanted to stay exactly where she was and wake up to see her mother in the living room watching Johnny Carson. Elvira took a deep breath. "Thank you," she said. "I appreciate all you've done." There, she'd said it. Sure enough, Mrs. Macy smiled, more warmly this time, and collected her notebook and sweater. The door clicked shut behind her.

Alone, Elvira shut her eyes and let the great, gasping sobs come. She leaned back in the lounge chair as waves of desolation swept over her. Who in the whole wide world cared about her? Was there one person? Elvira sobbed and sobbed.

In half an hour, Elvira was cried out. She felt weak. That was the last time, she told herself. No more self-pity. After going into the bathroom and splashing cold water on her face, she paced the living room rug and thought.

She could collect her clothes and go. Sneak out with the hundred dollars and stay in a hotel with a color TV and a swimming pool. Mrs. A. across the hall would never notice. Elvira happened to know that Mrs. Axtehelm sat in her dusty living room all afternoon drinking pink wine and watching soap operas. By four-thirty, her head was weaving like a dandelion on its stalk.

Elvira twisted a strand of her long black hair and rubbed it under her nose like a moustache, an old habit when she was thinking. Probably they'd find her the minute she tried to buy a bus ticket or rent a room. She was trapped. She had to get on the train for Charlottesville, Virginia—the place that Laureen had laughed at. "The sticks, honey. You heard of the sticks? Folks there just sit and watch the grass grow and listen to the frogs clear their throats. To them, that's excitement." Laureen would laugh and shake her head. "And that Carrie, hiding all her life back in those woods. What kind of life is that?"

But that hadn't stopped Laureen for one minute, had it, when it came to sending her own daughter right back there? Elvira gritted her teeth. She was too mad to cry now.

She stood up and looked around the living room. What should she take? Her throws from India. They would go. Across the sofa and tucked around the lounge chair were her blue-and-green-and-gold India print squares, big as bedspreads. Throws was what Laureen called them. Elvira called them tapestries. She picked them up, uncovering the flesh-colored upholstery they had hidden. Hideous.

9

Elvira hated ugly, flashy colors. That's why she'd spent her money buying the tapestries last year. She couldn't stand what that evil pink upholstery was saying to her every day. It was saying, "Here you are, Elvira Judson, an ordinary person in an ordinary place with nothing tomorrow or yesterday." The tapestries whispered about night and stars and soft winds with flowers and peacocks and tigers.

Elvira folded the tapestries and set them on the end of the sofa. Her incense burner would go too, and the carved statue that was probably ivory. Her peacock feathers she'd have to leave; there was no way to fit them in the suitcase. Her clothes were easier. Jeans and tops and one dress. Sneakers and dress shoes.

Elvira's taste was the opposite of Laureen's. Her mother liked pinks and purples and clothes everybody noticed right away. Elvira's clothes were quiet as water, green and blue and gray. There really weren't that many of them. Tomorrow she'd just add the last things—her toothbrush, her nightgown, the clothes she had on. One big case and one medium box tied with string. Elvira carried them into the living room and put them by the door.

2

HEY'LL GIVE you a pillow on the train. Maybe you'll sleep most of the way. You should just be getting into the pretty part of the trip around dawn, coming through the mountains in West Virginia," Mrs. Macy said the next afternoon in the train station coffee shop, crumpling her napkin and pushing back her chair.

Elvira resented the kind tone Mrs. Macy used. Nobody *really* cared about her. If anybody did, Elvira would not be sitting across from a lady who was paid to pretend to care about her.

Elvira pushed her plate away and reached for her pocketbook. "I'd like to pay for this," she said, "to thank you for all you've done."

Mrs. Macy looked startled. Elvira took the check before she could even reach for it and walked to the cash register. She handed the girl one of her five-dollar bills. When she got the change, she walked back and left fifty cents for a tip. Laureen had always complained about stingy tippers.

"Really, dear," Mrs. Macy said, "let me pay you back. It's city money, Elvira. Neither of us needs to pay."

Elvira flushed. The city of Chicago was not turning her into a charity case. She shook her head and shut her pocketbook.

Mrs. Macy was flustered as they walked down to the train. "Your aunt is going to call me tomorrow to let me know everything is all right," she said, "but let me hear from you too, will you?"

Elvira looked down the length of silver train, curving along the track as far as she could see. She shivered at the thought of getting on. She hadn't even called up Jennifer. She'd been afraid she'd break down. Now as she turned to Mrs. Macy to say goodbye, she found she was even sorry to leave *her* behind. She tossed her head. Hair floated around her face. "Good-bye," she said.

"Where to, miss?" asked the conductor, standing by the door in the little cloud of steam that hissed up from under the car.

"Charlottesville," Mrs. Macy said. "Charlottesville, Virginia."

"Five cars down, please," the man said. "Number fifteen."

Pulling open the door to car 15, Elvira turned and made herself smile at Mrs. Macy. "Good-bye," she said. "And thank you." She climbed on and let the door hiss shut behind her. Turning to the right, she pulled at the door to the car. The lights were on; the car was bright. Elvira found a seat on the side away from where Mrs. Macy was standing and leaned back, waiting to feel the car pull away.

An old lady was sitting across from her, still as a bird, her hands folded and her feet side by side on the footrest. A grandmother, Elvira thought, off to visit with her grandchildren. Elvira used to want a grandmother. Back when she was eight or so, when Laureen forgot about her half the time, Elvira had made up a grandmother. Grandmothers were pure love, Elvira thought with a sigh, just pure love. Getting presents for you and all.

Laureen had never gotten her presents much. Just once or twice. When Elvira was four years old, Laureen had gotten her a battery-operated doll that was advertised on TV. Laureen had loved the commercials of that doll, waving its arms and moving its mouth. So she bought it for Elvira's birthday. When she put the batteries in and turned it on, the doll made a shrill, humming noise, whirring along like an electric mixer. Its arms moved up and down and its mouth jerked open and shut. Elvira had screamed and dropped it.

"Eight dollars and ninety-five cents, and that one throws it on the floor!" Laureen had said for years afterward. "That's gratitude for you. Cute as a bug, and that one throws it on the floor."

Now Elvira did jobs, baby-sitting and cleaning and running to the store for people. She had her own money. Even so, sometimes she would pretend that something she had bought was really a present from her grandmother or her father. She liked to think that her father had given her the ivory statue.

Elvira sighed. A deep, sad feeling came over her whenever she thought about her father. People must be looking at her, thinking, *There's a sad look to that dark-haired girl over there. Some tragedy must have occurred in her past.*

Deserted twice—that was tragedy enough. Elvira thought again, as she had the day before, about her father's leaving

13

them. She had been only a baby. "Just cut and ran, leaving me with all the responsibility," Laureen had said to her fifty dozen times. Elvira knew well enough that she was the reponsibility her mother had gotten stuck with. Laureen had tried to sue for support money, but she never could find him. Nobody ever had. That was what had given Elvira the idea she'd had ever since she was a child.

Suppose he'd had a severe head injury? Lost his memory? Then he couldn't possibly remember his baby daughter. Oh, Elvira knew it wasn't exactly likely. Amnesia wasn't all that common. Nobody she knew had ever had it. But on soap operas, the kind she used to watch with Laureen, it happened all the time.

Sometimes, Elvira would work out a story like the ones on TV, about her father and herself and his suddenly recovering and remembering about her and rushing back to find her. It made her feel good, and it was practice for writing her novels later, when she was older.

Elvira thought of that hospital soap opera she and Laureen used to watch, the one where men and women doctors fell in love even though they were already married. Sometimes they had babies by mistake, and when the babies got sick, they checked the blood type and everybody found out who the real father was. Even though the plots were silly, they reminded Elvira of her own life. Those scenes where the real father was revealed and everybody broke down and cried made her cry, too. In one soap opera, a girl was sixteen before she found out who her real father was.

Elvira first saw her father, or the person she thought of as her father, on one of those soap operas. He was a doctor, and he looked right into her eyes. Elvira started thinking about him a lot, adding details. Some ideas she got from the paperbacks that came every month from Laureen's book club, "novels of romantic suspense." Every month Elvira read the new one before her mother did. Details from those books slipped into her thoughts about her imagined family and into the stories she wrote down in a private notebook. Writing every day was important to someone who planned to be a novelist, she'd once heard on a talk show.

Charlottesville was where her real father used to live. She might see him again. In Laureen's books, that was what happened. Long-lost parents and children always discovered each other. They always knew each other at a glance even though it had been twenty years since they'd met and one of them had been a baby at the time. Elvira stretched out in her seat, smiling.

The old lady across from her got up and stumbled toward the washroom, catching onto the seats as she went by. A waiter came through and announced that there was a snack bar four cars down. Elvira looked out the window at people who were having normal afternoons, and felt how strange it was that she was here, moving past them and their lives.

After an hour or so, Elvira began to feel hungry. Maybe a Coke and some ice cream would be good. She got up and started back through the cars. Some people were already starting to settle down to sleep, stretched out in their seats. Many of them leaned against the windows or curled up in the aisle seats, their heads sticking out from the armrests. She carefully avoided bumping into them. Lots of little children were lying against their parents, asleep. A few older ones knelt on the seats to stare out windows, and dashed up and down the aisles to the water coolers and toilets.

She bumped through the door to the snack bar, blinking in the sudden brightness of the fluorescent lights. A man in a white jacket was wiping off the counter. Eight or ten people were scattered around the tables beyond him. Four teen-age kids sat together playing cards and laughing. Elvira shrank into herself. Suddenly she felt conspicuous.

"Help you?" asked the man.

Elvira took her Coke and ice cream cup to an empty table and sat down. She looked at the empty chair across from her and imagined that a distinguished-looking gentleman, a passenger from those sleeping compartments she'd just passed, was standing beside her, smiling politely, asking if he might sit down. The scene started to take shape while Elvira sat staring out the window, drinking her Coke.

"Excuse me, miss," the tall, distinguished gentleman with gray sideburns and a three-piece suit said in a deep but friendly voice. "Is this seat taken?"

"Why no," Elvira replied, reserved but friendly, seeing that he was a complete gentleman in every way.

As they sat there, they began a polite conversation, the way travelers will, about where they were going and so forth. When Elvira said her destination was Charlottesville, the tall man gave a start, and a look of pain crossed his dark eyes. He drummed his long, surgeon's fingers on the table top and stared over her head into space, as if he were holding back strong feelings.

16

"Charlottesville . . ." he said, a yearning tone creeping into his manly voice. "So long ago . . ."

"You lived there?" Elvira asked, sensing there were painful yet pleasant memories about the place for him. She had barely met him, but in some mysterious way she felt she had known this distinguished stranger all her life.

She put her own hand flat down on the table, beside her Coke. This time there was no mistake. A look of wonder crossed the man's face as his eyes fixed on the tiny mark Elvira had just above her right wrist, an almost heart-shaped spot that she had been born with—her birthmark.

"It can't be," the man said, almost stammering. "It's impossible, and yet . . . I think . . . Your name, child? Your name couldn't be Elvira?"

Elvira's eyes were shining. She was just about to tell him that she was, she *really* was, the Elvira he had been seeking, when she was interrupted.

"Mind if I sit here?"

A man who looked a little like Duane was standing by the seat across from her. Elvira checked the other tables; they were filling up.

"That's OK," she said, flustered. The man was holding a plastic glass of beer. His fingers were plump and dark hair sprouted around his knuckles.

"Hot as blazes," he said, sitting down. He took a swallow of beer. "Air conditioning off in half the train." He used his paper napkin to wipe off his round, oily face. "Where you headed?"

"I'm going to Washington, D.C., to visit my sister," Elvira said. She didn't want to tell this man anything about herself.

17

Hands were a sign of a person's character, she'd read. Her father had surgeon's hands.

Elvira sipped her Coke. She wanted to finish it as soon as she could and get back to her seat. Suddenly there was an awful noise as she sucked air into her straw. She turned red.

"You could use a refill," the man said. "Let me get you another Coke. I'm going for another beer."

"No," Elvira said hastily. "No, thank you. I have to get back to my seat."

The man laughed. "Relax," he said. "My intentions are honorable. You know"—he leaned forward—"I bet I've got a kid just about your age. A daughter. How old are you?"

"Thirteen."

"Thirteen," he said thoughtfully, rolling his eyes for a second, as if he were figuring out his own daughter's age. "That's right. My girl's twelve and a half. And I got a boy four. Family man, that's me. So let me get you another Coke."

"No. Thank you, but I have to get back to my seat. My dad said I shouldn't stay long." She stood up. "Thank you anyway. Have a nice trip."

Back in her seat, Elvira leaned her head against the window and looked out. She cupped her hands around her eyes and saw trees close to the tracks; beyond them lay fields and woods. The man with the beer had jolted Elvira back to reality. She was a deserted daughter going to stay with an old aunt back in the bushes, and she might as well start facing up to it.

Elvira sat back and tried to imagine what Aunt Carrie looked like. Laureen had shown her some blurry snapshots. One of them Elvira remembered especially. Aunt Carrie was standing next to a tree in front of a porch. She'd moved one hand just as the picture was snapped, and there was a little blur. She had looked to Elvira like the sort of person who hates to have her picture taken, who feels foolish standing still in front of a shutter. Carrie was wearing the kind of dress country people might order out of a catalogue—no particular style. But she was smiling and looking in a friendly way at whoever was taking the picture. Just an ordinary-looking woman in a housedress.

When Laureen had muttered about how boring life in Virginia was, she'd talked about Carrie once in a while. Laureen had told her that Carrie worked in a clinic in town and lived in the old family house thirty miles outside of Charlottesville. "Invalids and raccoons and possums—that's all that woman sees from one day to the next!" Laureen had exclaimed. "Always in that hospital or off in the woods. *I* couldn't stand it, I tell you!"

Elvira couldn't figure out what had happened to make Laureen so down on Virginia. Vaguely, she felt it had to do with whatever Laureen had done to drive her father away. If you feel guilty about something, it just makes you act as if you hated everything connected with that thing. Elvira had noticed that in herself once or twice. Add that to Laureen's still being a waitress when she had hoped to become an actress, and Elvira could see why her mother might feel uneasy talking about her Aunt Carrie. Carrie had tried to persuade her to be a secretary, but Laureen had been sure that if she came to Chicago someone would recognize her talents.

Laureen made it plain that Aunt Carrie didn't have any imagination. "Just as ordinary as crabgrass and plain as tap water," she had said. Elvira felt a chill come over her.

She did not want to go to Charlottesville, left behind while Laureen and Duane went tootling off to Nashville. Elvira was sure that's where they went. It had been Laureen's dream to see Graceland, the former home of Elvis Presley. Elvira had assumed that when Laureen went, she'd go too. Any normal daughter would have thought that.

It was pitch-dark outside now. Elvira stretched across both seats and slept. She woke at little towns in Ohio when the train stopped. Once or twice she peered out at the lighted space in the stations, watched the people kissing good-bye beside their cars, hurrying along with their suitcases. Then she slept some more.

They pulled into Charlottesville at ten o'clock the next morning. The red-brick station, framed by pine trees, had white columns. It was small. Compared to Chicago, it was minute.

Elvira got off and looked apprehensively along the track. One of the people waiting there had to be her Aunt Carrie.

"Elvira? Are you Elvira Judson?" She turned. A middle-aged woman with gray hair pulled into a knot was smiling at her. She was efficient-looking. Like a retired gym teacher.

"Aunt Carrie?"

The lady pulled her close and hugged her. Elvira felt numb. She pulled back and made herself smile.

"Thank you for having me." Suddenly she was tongue-tied, standing on the platform beside this woman who kept smiling at her.

"Why, don't be silly. Having you? You're family. Where else're you going to go?" Aunt Carrie spoke rapidly, but with that drawn-out sound to the words—*faaamly*—that Elvira heard in Laureen's voice sometimes. Suddenly Elvira felt even more alone. People even talked differently here.

"Where're your bags, honey?" Aunt Carrie asked.

"Mrs. Macy checked them." Elvira squared her shoulders. She was glad to start on something practical.

They carried the bags to the parking lot and loaded them into Aunt Carrie's old red pickup. They climbed in, bumped out of the lot and headed down the street.

Elvira rolled down the window. A cool breeze blew in, fanning her hair out behind her.

3

HE DRIVE to Aunt Carrie's took almost an hour. Beside
the twisting road were signs with crooked arrows and
SLOW on them. Elvira smelled the cool scent of clay and pine
needles.

"Doubt if you remember much about the old place," Aunt
Carrie said after a while. "You were such a little thing when
you left."

"No," Elvira answered, looking out the window, trying to see
into the woods. "Not much of anything, really." She was used to
sidewalks and streets. These bushy woods full of vines were
frightening. Elvira rolled the window most of the way up again.

"Probably better get used to saying *ma'am*, Elvira honey. Not
that it makes much never mind to me, but you'll find people
here setting store by that sort of thing." Carrie smiled. "Might
as well get you off on the right foot, hadn't we? You'll be meeting the whole family this evening. They're dying to see you. I

hope you aren't too worn out from the trip because I had to tell them to come over for dinner. No way around it, they had to get a look at you. And we can't have people thinking you've been raised a Yankee, can we?"

Elvira's eyes widened. She hadn't known there were more relatives. And thinking she was a Yankee? That's what she *was*, if she was anything. Not some hillbilly, drawling through her nose. "That will be all right," she said, quietly. "I guess."

Aunt Carrie patted her knee. "Don't let it worry you, honey. You'll be a celebrity. Don't let all the attention go to your head, that's all. In a week, you'll just be one of the family. That's the way it works around here." Aunt Carrie wrestled the truck around a tight curve and shifted down for a steep grade. "I saved you the afternoon, Ellie, to get settled and rest if you like. That was the best I could do."

People clamoring to meet her. That was something that had never occurred to Elvira. She'd felt uneasy just thinking of Aunt Carrie and Cousin Henry. How many more were there? Would they be asking about Laureen? So far, Carrie hadn't said one word about her mother. Elvira took a deep breath. She ought to be the first to mention it. "Laureen got married," she said.

"So the lady from your school mentioned, Elvira. Kind of sudden, wasn't it?" A tight quality came into her voice. Elvira sensed her disapproval. To her surprise, she felt some loyalty to her mother.

"She'd let me know it was happening," she lied. "More or less. It wasn't a complete surprise, exactly."

"Well, it was lucky for us, Elvira. I have been wanting to have you out to stay for years. Your mamma talk much about the family, Elvira? Tell you about life back in these woods?"

"She said she never wanted to come back," Elvira blurted out. She chewed her lip. Why had she said such a dumb thing?

Aunt Carrie chuckled. "The movie star. Always had big plans, Laureen did. Packing her suitcase by the age of nine. But don't let Laureen think for you, child. You look to have a head on your shoulders."

"Plain as tap water," Laureen's voice spoke right in Elvira's ear. "That Carrie has always been dishwater simple." Elvira squirmed. *She* was a person with plans, too.

"You are nice to have me," she said.

"I'm real anxious to get to know you, Elvira. Glad to have the chance. With me, blood counts. Family, stretching back into the past, forward into the future. Simpsons and Peytons and Marshalls." Carrie turned off the road suddenly, bumping onto a rutted gravel drive. The truck lurched around two curves before they got to a cleared space. They were at a stand of oak trees and an old yellow house with a sagging porch across the front. "Try to get away from it like Laureen did, if you want to," Aunt Carrie said, as she stopped the truck. "Turn your back on it all you want, but still that's what you are—all those names and all this red clay and Scotch broom and honeysuckle."

They climbed out of the truck and walked around to get Elvira's bags. Five or six cats came spilling off the porch, with two reddish hounds.

"Sam," Aunt Carrie said, pointing to the dog with a white streak on his face, "and Thomas." She reached down and patted Thomas. "I doubt if you and Laureen had a pair of coon hounds the equal of these off in Chicago." She laughed and opened the tailgate, pulling out Elvira's bags. "Come on in, honey. See the old place."

Next to the porch a mimosa tree was in bloom. The air was full of the exotic sweet smell. Elvira felt the strangeness of the place, of herself carrying her clothes across this saggy porch with skinny hound dogs snaking past her. Tears stung her eyes, but she blinked them back.

"Your cousin Henry is living with me now," Aunt Carrie said. "I don't remember if I wrote Laureen. Past eighty years old now. Getting too old to do for himself. He's dying to see you, but let's just get you settled into your room. Then you can come down and meet Henry and I'll show you around."

The staircase stood behind the front door; Elvira followed Carrie up. On the second floor were another central hall and three rooms—one big and two small. "This was Laureen's room," Aunt Carrie said, carrying her bag into one of the small ones. "Seemed like it ought to be yours now."

Aunt Carrie showed her the closet and pulled open a bureau drawer to make sure she'd emptied it. "I'll leave you to get yourself unpacked, Elvira. Let me know if you need anything." She went downstairs.

Elvira looked at the room. There was no trace of Laureen. A few stains like streaks of tea drizzled down one flowered wall. An iron bed painted white with little knobs and twirls on it, and an old bureau with glass knobs and a starched runner on top. Rag rugs on the floor. It was a homely little country bedroom— what she would have guessed a room in Aunt Carrie's house would look like. Plain and ordinary. Dishwater simple. Laureen's mocking voice sounded in her ears again. "That Carrie is just dishwater simple."

Elvira sat on the bed and tried to imagine her mother in Carrie's house. The room was quiet, shadowy, and smelled cool.

Thoughts of the past seemed natural. Summers, when she was a girl, Laureen used to come for long visits with Carrie, she'd told Elvira. Her mother, Carrie's sister, had made her. "Poor Carrie isn't the marrying kind. Won't have any little girls of her own," Laureen's mother had said. Elvira's grandmother had died off in Kentucky when Elvira was four. Kind of a teary lady, squishy like a sofa pillow—that's all Elvira could remember of her. The opposite of her sister almost. Aunt Carrie was so sensible and take-charge. No wonder she had gotten the reputation for being so dependable. Laureen had said, "Always helping this one or that one. That Carrie never figured out how to have a life of her own."

Well, that sure wasn't Laureen's problem, was it? "You want a life of your own, Laureen?" she muttered. "Don't let me stand in your way. Just dump your daughter, hear?"

Elvira walked to the window and peered out at the yard. What was it that made Laureen so determined to stay away from this place? They'd lived here once, after all, even though Elvira couldn't remember a thing. For a whole year, until she was two. Her father had left when Elvira was a year old, and it was then that Laureen had come out to stay with Carrie. "And you won't see me back there, I tell you. That's one place that has seen all of me it's going to!" Laureen's voice again. Maddening the way that kept happening, Elvira thought. She didn't need to be reminded of her mother by hearing her voice all the time.

She looked more closely at the scene out the window. The sun was high. In the white heat the yard seemed to be waiting. Nothing moved. Elvira shivered. At home she could see people passing, cars pulling up to the curb. She heard voices calling, doors banging, horns beeping. Here every blade of grass, every bush, sat frozen. The rose bushes weren't clipped; they just grew naturally, long thorny arches sticking up beside the barn.

The grass was cut, though, and there was a vegetable garden, with two rows of zinnias and sweet peas along the edge. Elvira knew the names of a few flowers. Jennifer's mother grew some beside their house. Elvira thought of their garden, a civilized row of petunias, troweled and pretty. Here things grew on their own.

Beyond the yard and the garden there was a barn and then the woods. It was the same tangle of honeysuckle, bushes and trees that had lined the road all the way from town. The country in Illinois was nothing like this. Farms, mostly. Big, fat barns and silos with plowed fields. A few patches of woods, maybe, but not dark and twisted with vines. Off in the distance, Elvira saw trees rise steeply, become the base to a mountain. "These woods," Aunt Carrie had called them. Dark walls shutting off the sky. Elvira felt like a princess in a fairy story shut up in a tower, surrounded by dark trees and wild wilderness and snakes and frogs.

She shut her eyes for a second, blotting out the strangeness of the outside. The room was almost a relief after the view from the window. Getting out her clothes, shaking out her own shirts and jeans to hang them in the empty closet, Elvira relished the sense of what belonged to her. She put her India spreads in a bottom drawer, not sure she wanted to see them yet in this room. They would look as odd as she felt. She put the incense burner in the drawer, too.

27

There wasn't much to unpack, but Elvira worked slowly, giving herself a chance to be alone. After she had shoved the suitcase under the bed, she sighed and went downstairs.

"And here's the little lady now!" A booming voice greeted her as she entered the big kitchen.

A white-haired old man with a big hooked nose and close-set blue eyes was sitting in a wheelchair, his lap covered with an afghan. "Little Cousin Elvira!" he exclaimed as she came up to him to shake hands. He held her hand and smiled up at her. "Beautiful. Isn't she beautiful, Carrie? Like all the Peyton women—every one of them!"

He *looked* eighty years old. That's what Aunt Carrie had said he was. And crippled besides. Elvira wriggled her fingers out of his grasp, startled and a little frightened. Henry turned her loose at once, and suddenly she felt embarrassed. She hadn't wanted to hurt his feelings.

"It's nice to meet you, Cousin Henry," she said hesitantly. He was a big man, or had been. The bones in his face were prominent, not just his nose, but his chin and his cheekbones, too. And his hands were big, with long fingers, knotted now with arthritis. He held his shoulders square and there was a sort of military straightness about him, even sitting.

"Don't be silly, honey!" he said. "An old wreck like me! Don't blame you for backing off. Shouldn't have grabbed you like that. Keep forgetting what an old crow I've turned into!" He smiled at her, the wrinkles deepening around his eyes, making that blue stare less intense.

Elvira started to lie politely, but she suddenly felt something stir inside her. His expression had more pure kindness in it than

28

she had ever seen anywhere. She just smiled down at him, feeling awkward.

"Just as sweet as she is pretty," Cousin Henry said to Aunt Carrie. "I tell you, I am blessed, spending my last days surrounded by beautiful ladies."

Carrie laughed. "Elvira isn't going to have her head turned by your foolishness, Henry. Ellie has a mind of her own—anybody can see that." Carrie turned back to the sink, where she was cutting up chickens. She already had a pile of legs and breasts on the pan next to her, enough to feed an army.

"Can I help, Aunt Carrie?" Elvira asked.

"Sure can, honey," Aunt Carrie said. "We're going to need some peas. Think you could go out back and pick us a good mess of peas? Yesterday when I checked, there were plenty ready." She handed Elvira a colander.

Elvira had never picked any vegetables, except out of a bin at the grocery store, but she wasn't going to give Carrie the chance to talk about "city girls." How complicated could picking peas be?

In the garden she'd seen from her bedroom window, Elvira looked up and down the bushy rows of plants for something with peas on it. They were vines, twisting over strings stretched from poles at the end of each row. Elvira waded in and pulled at a fat pod. The vine tore. Sweat started to drip down her face, making her blink. Elvira pulled her shirt up and wiped her face. She stooped and tried again, using both hands and twisting the pea pod off the vine instead of pulling. Down the row she went, reaching in for the fat pods, twisting them off, dropping them in the colander.

Almost at the end of the first row, she stopped to listen, hearing the buzzing noise of a motorbike off in the woods beyond the field. It came in sight, only about twenty feet away, a blue moped with a blond boy riding it. For a second he swerved, surprised to see her. He stared at her, then disappeared into the woods again. Elvira looked after him, disappointed that he hadn't stopped. He looked about sixteen. She went back to the peas.

"Nice job, honey," Aunt Carrie said when she came in. "You're not such a city girl after all."

"You hear that dirt bike back there?" Cousin Henry asked. "You didn't see that scamp that was riding it, did you?" He was agitated; his blue eyes glared.

"Now, Henry," Aunt Carrie said, frowning. "No need to excite yourself over nothing."

"*Nothing?*" Henry said. "You have a peculiar definition of nothing. A mighty peculiar definition of nothing."

"I saw him," Elvira said. "A blond boy. Who is he? Does he live around here?"

Cousin Henry leaned forward. "Michael Andrews, that's his name. But we don't speak it in this house. That sneak."

"Henry, you ought to go on the stage," Aunt Carrie said, "instead of wasting all that drama just on Ellie and me." She made a little face at him. Elvira could see that she was telling him not to make so much stir around her. She wondered what they were steering her away from.

"He just looked like a kid," Elvira said. "What's so awful about him?"

Cousin Henry leaned back in his chair and quieted down a little. "For one thing," he said, "riding that buzz-saw bicycle of his past my pea patch. Defiling the peace and quiet with that motorized contraption. Did you hear me invite him over here?" He was getting overwrought again. "I issued no such invitation. The sheriff will be informed."

"Let's not bother Jimmy with trifles," Carrie said. "Give him his Sunday. Don't you mention this to him when he comes by."

"Who is Jimmy?" Elvira asked.

"Cousin Louise's husband," Aunt Carrie said. "And he's the sheriff, too. They have a daughter—your cousin Ellen Rose—just your age. But we've got no call to be taking advantage of him when he's out socially." She frowned at Henry. He adjusted his afghan and wheeled himself out the door to the front porch. "Henry overreacts," Carrie whispered to Elvira. "Don't let it worry you. Nothing to it but old age."

Elvira thought there was more to it, but she was willing to let it drop. Probably Michael had run over some green beans or something. Living out here, away from everything, Aunt Carrie and Cousin Henry probably thought every tiny thing was super important. Michael was a good-looking boy; he was certainly the most interesting person she'd seen so far. If she pressed them further about him, they might tell her she shouldn't speak to him if he came past again. Elvira didn't want that.

"Are Cousin Louise and Jimmy coming over?" she asked, changing the subject. "Are they some of the people coming for dinner?"

"Yes. They're coming. Everybody's coming. You've got cousins behind every bush in this county. Never knew that, did you? And, like I said, once they heard you'd be here, there was no holding them off."

Elvira sighed. She dreaded all these strangers clustering

31

around her. "How many will there be?" she asked in a small voice.

Aunt Carrie laughed and patted her on the shoulder. "Land, child, you don't need to worry. I didn't mean to scare you off. Twenty or so, I guess, in all. But they're just family, Elvira. *Your* family! You keep that in mind."

"Laureen never mentioned our having so many cousins. Just you and Cousin Henry."

"Well, honey, as you said in the truck, Laureen decided to leave all this behind—find herself a new life." She peered at Elvira. "And I'm not saying that's bad. Laureen didn't have an easy time. And everybody wants something different out of life, isn't that so?"

Elvira nodded. She wondered what Aunt Carrie meant exactly by saying that Laureen hadn't had an easy time. Could she find out something more about her father? Elvira hesitated. Something held her back. Today, she told herself, wasn't a good time to go into that. Carrie was bustling around the kitchen, flouring the chicken, getting out heavy iron frying pans.

"Maybe you could get going on shelling those peas, Elvira, if you would? We stand around much longer talking, we aren't going to have any dinner when they get here."

Elvira sat on the stool Aunt Carrie pulled up for her and started shelling the peas, watching them bounce when they hit the bottom of the metal bowl. Here she was in this strange kitchen, shelling peas as if she lived here. And just yesterday at about this time she was getting on the train at home. Elvira blinked back tears of homesickness.

In a day or two, Laureen would be sending her a postcard, Elvira thought, clenching her teeth. It would probably rave on about her wonderful trip and about how much she missed her precious daughter. Elvira squeezed the next pod so hard she smashed one end. She took a deep breath and slowed down. Carefully, she watched as her fingers shelled the peas, scraped them from the pods and sent them plumping into the bowl.

"Nice job, honey!" Aunt Carrie exclaimed. "I can just see you're going to fit right in."

4

*A*UNT CARRIE was right—Elvira had never suspected she had so many relatives. Cars came bumping down the lane starting at six o'clock. Aunt Carrie's porch was crowded by six-thirty. Ellen Rose, the cousin who was her age, was a spindly thing with yellow hair and a peaked-looking, bony face and green eyes. She stared at Elvira until Elvira felt like some kangaroo in a cage. Elvira swallowed and tried to act nice.

Later they both helped to carry platters of fried chicken, Jell-O salad and biscuits out to the porch where Aunt Carrie had set up a long table. Elvira was juggling a big platter of sliced tomatoes and cold ham, walking behind Ellen Rose. As she left the kitchen, Ellen Rose gave the swinging door an extra push. Elvira barely turned sideways in time to take it on her shoulder rather than the plate.

Ellen Rose's snake eyes glittered at her, hoping to see Elvira

34

covered with watery tomato seeds and ham grease. *Some cousin,* Elvira thought.

"They feed you like this off in Chicago, Elvira honey?" one of the men, Cousin Fred, said as she came onto the porch. "You get this southern fried chicken, these feathery biscuits out where you were?" Elvira thought about the Colonel Sanders half a block down the street where Laureen used to buy half their Sunday dinners. She smiled.

"Just put that down there, honey, and come stand by me." One of the women at the table cleared a space, making room for the platter. Elvira stuck her knuckle in the potato salad. Embarrassed, she stood there with mayonnaise on her hand.

"I declare, let me look at you," the lady said. It was Cousin Louise, Ellen Rose's mother. "Look at this girl, Jimmy," she said. "Isn't she a picture? Honey, we're all so glad to have you," she whispered in Elvira's ear, giving her arm a squeeze. "Ellen Rose is so lucky to have a cousin just her age. You-all are going to be like sisters before long!"

"It's nice of Aunt Carrie to have me," Elvira said. Ellen Rose, standing across the porch, simpered.

"Nonsense, sugar," Cousin Jimmy said. He was a big man, with legs too long for Carrie's rickety lawn chair. He looked like a grasshopper sitting there. "You'll be a big help to Carrie and Henry. A godsend to those two." He smiled up at her.

Elvira knew they were all thinking about how Laureen had gone off and deserted her. The minute her back was turned, they'd probably all be saying how sad it was that she'd been dumped on Carrie this way. Here was Ellen Rose, safe in her family, with a father who was the sheriff—somebody everyone was bound to look up to—and it was clear what *she* thought of Elvira.

"Ellen Rose used to love to visit out here," Cousin Louise said. "I had to drag her home after a week most summers. Given the chance, she would have moved right in." She blinked, as Elvira looked away.

"Exploring back in those woods." Jimmy laughed. "That little girl used to spend hours roaming around those woods, building dams on the creek, one thing and another. How are you for hiking in the woods, Elvira? Are you the outdoors type?"

"How could she be, Daddy?" Ellen Rose had come over next to them. She put her hand on her father's shoulder. "She's a city girl. Elvira is a stranger to these mountains. She's probably afraid she'd meet up with a bear or a snake." Ellen Rose laughed.

"We have woods in Illinois," Elvira said. "I used to walk in the woods a lot." What a lie, she thought. She looked at the floor, disgusted with herself.

"Those Yankee woods aren't like *these* woods," Ellen Rose said sweetly. "You don't even have snakes up north."

"You don't call Chicago north," Cousin Jimmy said. "It's more west. The Midwest. Where's your geography, Ellen Rose?"

"I was planning to go out and walk around in the woods some tomorrow," Elvira said suddenly. "I thought it would be interesting to see what it's like."

"Good for you, sugar," Cousin Jimmy said. "Show a little spunk. Take hold, now you're here." He looked pleased. Ellen Rose looked droopy. Elvira smiled. Wiping the smear of salad off her finger with a napkin, she went to the other side of the

36

porch to talk to two old ladies perched side by side on the lawn glider. More cousins.

All that family was like a huge net, closing in around her, Elvira thought lying in bed that night and staring at the ceiling. "Hasn't she got the Marshall nose?" Cousin Susan had exclaimed. "Isn't that gorgeous black hair pure Simpson?" some other lady had gushed.

"The girl is Peyton through and through," Cousin Henry had told them, his blue eyes glistening with emotion. "She's the image of her great-grandmother, Carrie's mother," he had said later that afternoon when Carrie was out of earshot. "It's as if we had that angel back among us." Hearing this, Cousin Jimmy had stirred uneasily and patted Henry on the shoulder.

"I am myself," Elvira had felt like saying. "I am myself. This is my nose and hair. I am not cousin anything. I am plain Elvira. Period."

But, of course, she hadn't. She had been polite until her face ached—even to that jealous snake Ellen Rose. Jealous like all green-eyed people—that's what Laureen would say.

Living with Laureen, Elvira never had to be stared at by cousins. She and Laureen kept off to themselves. That was what Elvira was used to. Tears blurred her eyes. She could almost hear Laureen's throaty laugh, almost see her peeling the polish off the tops of her nails the way she did when she watched the late movie. Elvira clenched her teeth. The whole thing was Laureen's fault. If she had been anything like a normal mother, Elvira wouldn't have been shoved off on these relatives back in the woods, drowning in cousins and aunts.

Being pitied was horrible. Elvira thrashed around under her

covers. All of them were bound to be feeling sorry for her, clucking their tongues and shaking their heads the way she'd seen two of them doing today when she came up behind them.

But then, Elvira told herself, Laureen's side wasn't her *real* family. Hadn't Laureen told her over and over that Elvira was the image of her father? For years Elvira had thought that was where her real ties were. Like him, Elvira was going to be a successful person out in the world by herself. Not trapped back in the bushes in Appalachia eating fried chicken. "To be yourself, you have to be free," Elvira whispered, shutting her eyes.

When Elvira woke up the next morning, she lay for a minute, looking at the leafy shadows on the wallpaper. Where was the noise? The drone of trucks and buses, the whine of motorcycles, the honking of horns? Elvira missed her morning sounds, resented the lemony light splashing on her walls, the calling of birds outside her window.

She looked outside. Seeing the woods past the garden, Elvira felt sick. She was supposed to walk around back there. Yesterday it had been the perfect way to flatten Ellen Rose. Today, she'd have to do it, actually hack her way into that jungle. Because one thing was certain—Ellen Rose was going to check up. She'd never let it drop, Elvira knew that.

Well, she thought, pulling on her jeans, what could be so terrifying back there anyway? Ellen Rose had spent half her childhood in the woods, to hear her parents talk, and that Michael Andrews boy was there yesterday. Snakes were normally afraid of people. She'd read that herself.

Elvira made up her bed, so nobody could say she was sloppy, and went down to breakfast. "Maybe I could go exploring, Aunt

Carrie," she said, pushing her egg with her toast. "Maybe I could go hiking in the woods out in back. I never got to do that, living in the city and all."

"Well, honey, I don't know," Aunt Carrie said, putting her coffee cup down carefully. "You've got to know what you're doing in the woods—watch out for snakes, that sort of thing."

Cousin Henry laughed. "Honestly, Carrie, I never thought I'd see the day you'd be warning children out of the woods. You that spent the first fifteen years of your life climbing trees and wading in the creek. You collected enough stuff for a museum!"

"But, Henry, I was used to the woods. It's all new to Elvira." Aunt Carrie started cleaning the table. "And you and I are going to town. She'll be by herself."

Cousin Henry looked thoughtful. "Maybe what our little lady wants is a little time alone. You've had a lot of changes lately, Elvira. Maybe you want to get off by yourself and take stock. I was like that. Liked to get off into the mountains and think about things."

Aunt Carrie sniffed. "The sooner everybody gets a grip on the here and now, the better. Dreaming and mooning around in the bushes just leads to problems."

Elvira smiled gratefully at Cousin Henry. It was hard to imagine him young, a dreamer. It was impossible to imagine Aunt Carrie ever being like that, even for a minute. Elvira watched her as she squeezed suds into the dishpan, getting ready to do the breakfast dishes almost before they'd finished with them. She'd never seen anybody that kept her eyes on what she was doing, that just went straight ahead, more than Aunt Carrie did. She never let her hands rest or her mind float, not as far as Elvira could see.

"I'll be fine. People go for hikes all the time," Elvira said, carrying her plate over and picking up a dish towel.

"Let her take the dogs, Carrie," Cousin Henry said. "There's nothing back there Sam and Thomas can't handle."

"Well, all right," Aunt Carrie said. "I guess you are right. I'm getting too fussy in my old age. Let's pack you a lunch and you can make a day of it." As soon as they finished the dishes, she started assembling waxed paper and sandwich makings. "Henry has his clinic appointment. And Monday, Wednesday and Friday afternoons I fill in at the clinic. Semiretired, but I don't like to lose touch. It'll be close to dinnertime before we get back. You're sure you want to stay? You could go into town and visit with Louise and Ellen Rose." Aunt Carrie pursed her lips; worry lines deepened around her mouth.

"I'll be fine here," Elvira said. "You just mention to Ellen Rose that I went for a walk in the woods. I'll see her another time."

The woods were dark and suddenly cool after the glare of the yard. Elvira looked to be sure the dogs were coming. "Sam! Thomas!" They snaked off into the bushes, noses to the ground. The air smelled musty and mysterious. Odd little creakings and chirps came from the bushes. Elvira stopped for a minute to get her bearings. She put her hand against the bark of a tree. Suddenly a little chip came alive and ran a foot or two up the trunk. She gasped and jumped back. A fingernail-sized toad sat partway up the tree trunk, wrinkled and gray-brown as the bark. "Yeah," she said, nastily. "I'm a Yankee. Not used to frogs on trees. Not planning to spend my life bushwhacking in Appalachia, either. You can count on that." The toad blinked, but it didn't move.

She walked on, swinging her lunch sack, half-whistling to reassure herself. She came to a path that seemed easy enough to follow. She had no idea where it might lead—deeper into nowhere, as far as she could see. Her hair swung against her shoulder blades and her sneakers made a soft swish as Elvira stepped along the path.

Farther in, there were more and more pine trees. Needles coated the path, making it slippery. Elvira was breathing easier, finding that the rhythm of walking, the freedom of being off by herself, was giving her some peace. Running and sliding on the needles would probably be fun, she thought. It was—the first time. The second, she fell over backward when she tried to stop.

"Go away, Thomas!" she hissed at the hound, who rushed over, lapping at her face.

"Wait until my dad hears I'm here," Elvira said, standing up. "He'll come to see about me. San Francisco. New York. Who knows where we might end up living?" Thomas cocked his ears forward, listening. Then he shook his head, flapping his ears, and ran off. Ever since the snack bar on the train, Elvira had thought more and more about her father. He was more real to her now than he had been for two or three years—since the time she'd gone to the hospital to have her appendix out.

Whenever she was scared or thought people were staring at her, Elvira thought of her father and his tweed jacket and his distinguished sideburns. That time in the hospital she had lain in bed and pictured him coming through the door, carrying a big bunch of red roses.

41

Now, brushing off the pine needles that stuck to the back of her jeans, feeling foolish, she saw him pulling up in his Cadillac Eldorado, heard the satisfying thump of the heavy car door swing shut as he closed it for her. The two of them, packed and leaving Aunt Carrie's for good, heading off for a life in a city somewhere—eating in restaurants most nights, going to plays and concerts. She'd send postcards to Aunt Carrie and Laureen, telling them about the kind of life she'd gone to, maybe even inviting them for visits. Why not?

But Aunt Carrie was such a plain sort of person. She probably wouldn't come. She was nice, *really* kind, not like Mrs. Macy, pretending to be. Elvira liked her. But still, she saw that Laureen was right. "Plain as tap water."

"Couldn't stand it here yourself, Laureen, so you decided to send me!" Elvira pressed her jaws together hard and held her breath. No crying, that was her rule.

There was a creek up ahead, where the path turned. Elvira heard the dogs splash and bark farther down, chasing something. Trees leaned over the creek and filtered the sunlight, making amber, wavy lines in the water. Elvira cupped her hands and splashed her face. The water was the color of pale Chinese tea and very cold. Long-legged bugs were racing across the surface, making lacy patterns from their shadows on the sandy bottom. Elvira watched them, getting her mind off her misery.

"Wharrf! Wharrf! Wharrf!" Those dogs were barking their heads off. Elvira peered down the path, trying to see. A few yards down, with a series of stepping stones, the path crossed the creek. She hesitated for a minute. Then she ran, jumping lightly from one stone to the other, heading for the dogs and whatever it was they were barking at. Once across, Elvira saw that the woods stopped a few yards ahead, where the sunlight glared down brightly beyond the trees. Maybe it was somebody's farm. She walked cautiously to the edge of the trees and peered out, blinking in the light.

Like a picture in a magazine, it was sitting in the weeds, an old plantation house, red brick and tall columns, its windows gaping empty with just a pane or two of glass here and there to catch the sun. Astonished, Elvira put her hand against the tree trunk next to her and stared. She touched paper. A notice was stapled to the tree—POSTED, it said, ending with PRIVATE PROPERTY. Elvira stepped out of the woods and looked toward the sound of the dogs.

The house was surrounded by big boxwood bushes. A figure came running from behind them, cutting across the field toward her.

"This property is posted," he called. "Can't you read the sign?"

Elvira took a step back, toward the shelter of the trees. The boy came panting up, red-faced from running. "What're you doing here?" he asked, stopping a few feet away and glaring at her.

"Nothing," Elvira said. "I'm not doing anything."

"Well, go do it someplace else," he snapped. "This is private property." He squinted, sort of swaying back on his heels and sticking out his chin.

"I know who you are," she said. "You're Michael Andrews."

"And you're Carrie's niece, come to stay," Michael answered roughly. "So what?" He stuck a stalk of grass in his mouth and chewed it. He stared at her, frowning. Michael was square and

43

solid, with muscled shoulders and short-fingered, broad hands. His hair stood up in a cowlick.

"You're sure super polite," Elvira snapped.

"That's right," Michael said, hitching up his jeans. "I'm famous for it."

"How come you're not in school?" she asked. "Isn't there school today?"

He frowned at her, wagging that grass in her face. She felt dumb. Obviously, he was skipping. Elvira looked over at the house, at the red brick glowing in the sun. "Can I look inside?" she asked.

"It's a free country." Michael threw the grass stalk away and spat over his shoulder to get rid of the bits in his mouth. He started walking across the field. Elvira followed.

"This isn't your house, is it?" Elvira asked. She immediately felt foolish. It was obviously too far gone for anybody to live in it.

"Where're you from again?" he asked. "The houses there must be in great shape!"

"Chicago," Elvira said defiantly. "I come from Chicago."

"No kidding?" Michael stopped dead in his tracks and stared at her, real interest in his expression. "You know the city and all?" He sounded almost respectful.

"I'd be pretty likely to, wouldn't I?" Elvira snapped, "living there?"

"Sure, sure," he said. He sounded distracted. He led her through a narrow space between boxwood bushes and they came up in front of the house.

5

GOING UP the steps, Elvira saw the wavy pattern in the fan-shaped window over the front door, shimmering like old silk. The doorknob was gone and the hinges creaked when Michael pushed the big door open. Inside, Elvira felt suddenly as if she had stepped into a church—the stillness, the sense of some special presence there, in the shadows, overwhelmed her.

A wide front hall ran the length of the house. A staircase curved gracefully midway up. The frozen curve of it, suspended there, heightened the feeling of time stopped. Elvira almost expected to see someone—a long-skirted lady, a frock-coated gentleman, a maid carrying a baby in a long lace dress—drift past one of the doors opening off the hall. Michael pulled at her elbow. They went into the room on the right.

"There used to be a mantelpiece there," Michael said, pointing to a scar around the fireplace opening. "Somebody ripped it off. Marble." Their steps echoed in the high-ceilinged spaces.

The walls were paneled partway up and painted white. Above the paneling hung patches of paisley wallpaper, a delicate blue and white. Someone had chosen that paper, had filled vases with daffodils and roses, had written invitations to balls in spidery handwriting, had suffered tragedies and fallen in love, all in this room. A room like this, a house like this, would elevate the most common things you could do, Elvira thought. If you sat in here and wrote a grocery list, hemmed a skirt, drank a cup of tea, there would still be a kind of importance, of poetry, about your life. Nobody could live here and just be a plain, ordinary person.

"You want to see the upstairs?" Michael asked, breaking the spell.

Elvira nodded. Walking into this house was like finding herself in one of those novels of Laureen's. Or like walking into one of the stories she'd started writing in her notebook.

"You have to stay close to the wall," Michael cautioned. "Some of the steps are loose."

There were five big bedrooms upstairs, two of them across the back of the house. They went into one and looked out the window. In back, a garden was going to weeds. Box hedges twined and curved in something like a maze. There were dogwood trees and a few daffodils and iris, past blooming, and one old rose vine meandering up the garden wall. The rest was weeds. The spikey iron fence in the back enclosed a small square, about the size of a room, and off to the right there was a one-room brick building.

"What's that?" Elvira asked.

"Summer kitchen," Michael said. "But we can't go in there," he added gruffly. "It's not safe."

"Why not?"

"Falling down." He looked away. "Bricks all loose. If you went in there, the whole thing might fall on you."

That didn't make sense. A one-story building? Elvira started to ask another question, but Michael was tilting his chin the way he had when he first came across the field. She dropped it. Having found this house, having walked inside it, Elvira was not about to make him mad. She wanted to come back here.

"This house is perfect," she said when they came back downstairs. "It is the most perfect house I ever saw."

"Needs a lot of fixing up," Michael said. "And would cost an arm and a leg to heat, that's for sure." Elvira remembered him zooming past on his dirt bike yesterday. Michael had a solid, practical look; he didn't fit the world of the house.

"You like it here?" she asked, hoping to find out something about him.

"It's OK," he said. "Quiet." His face shut in on itself. He wasn't going to talk. Not to her, anyway. "How'd you get here?" he asked. "Bus?"

"No," Elvira said. "I rode the train."

"Cost much?"

"About seventy dollars for coach," Elvira said. "Why? Are you planning to go to Chicago?"

"Naw," he said, looking nervous. "How could I do that?"

"Well, I don't know," Elvira said. "You just sounded interested, that's all."

"Interested don't mean I'm going. Lots of people are interested in things."

"That's true." Elvira sighed. Talking to this boy was work. He was always acting insulted or jumpy or something. One of those

47

boys who always swagger a little when they walk, the kind that lean up against their lockers at school and watch the girls, narrow-eyed.

"You check into the bus at all?" he asked. "I have a friend who might be heading out that way."

"No," Elvira said. "Somebody else made all the arrangements for me." That sounded almost elegant, as if she had a secretary or something. He didn't have to know it was a social worker, she thought, with the faintest twinge of guilt. "I'd like to look around out back," she said quickly, before he could ask anything else.

"Sure," Michael said, "come on." Their sneakers thudded softly on the bare floor as they walked across the drawing room to the French doors that opened onto the back porch. Up close, half-covered by weeds and ivy, the garden looked like part of a fairy tale.

"It's like the 'Sleeping Beauty' or something," Elvira said, pausing on the top step. "Hidden away here in the woods."

"You really go for that kind of stuff." Michael laughed. "You've been walking around bug-eyed ever since you came out of the woods. Say, what's your name? All this time, you never said what your name is."

"I'm sorry," Elvira said, blushing. "I forgot I knew your name but you don't know mine. It's Elvira. Elvira Judson."

Michael stared. "Elvira?" he said. "I don't believe it."

All her life Elvira had had to put up with dumb jokes about her name. It was the one thing that really made her mad. She liked her name, always had. It was probably the only time when Laureen's taste had been like hers. "Well, what about it?" she

48

snapped. "At least everybody you meet isn't named it, the way they are with *Michael!*"

"Hold on," Michael said. "You aren't getting it. You've got to see something you won't believe!" He caught her elbow and pulled her down into the garden. "This way." Elvira followed him, trotting along the brick path to the spikey iron fence she'd seen from the window. He pushed open the gate.

It was a family cemetery. A large pointed marker in the center of the plot had MATTHEWS carved on it, and seven or eight individual gravestones were scattered around it. Ivy had taken over the ground; most of the stones were partly covered by vines. "Is this where the family was buried?" Elvira asked. "The one that lived here?"

"Yeah," Michael said. He scrambled past the pointed marker to a smaller grave over by the fence. He pulled back some ivy to expose the inscription on the stone. "Look here," he said.

ELVIRA

Unmistakably, that was what it said. Elvira gasped and leaned closer.

ELVIRA
BELOVED DAUGHTER
1845–1863

She pulled the last tendril of ivy off the front of the stone and ran her fingers across the inscription, feeling the letters to believe them. Her own name. Suddenly Elvira understood why this house had seemed so perfect to her, why she had been so mysteriously at home in those echoing rooms. Never anywhere had she felt so *right* as she did in this house that seemed to come

49

from her own dreams. There was a plan behind it all, she realized now, connected to this name, Elvira. She sat down beside the grave and stared.

"Well, fire up," Michael said, grinning. "You're named for a ghost." He laughed and sat down by the fence. "People used to claim they saw her—seriously. That's how I happened to know she was buried back here. All the ghost talk."

"Have you ever seen her?"

"You've got to be kidding." Michael laughed and rubbed his head. "I'm not the type. That was a while back anyway. Before the road was moved, before the new highway, kids used to come out here a lot. Back when my parents, and I guess yours too, were in high school. They'd come here to make out. At night, of course. And some people claimed they'd seen her—this girl ghost."

"Has anybody seen her lately?"

"Naw. All that talk died down years ago. After the four-lane was finished, the road out was closed—a couple of trees blew across it. Now you have to walk all the way in. So nobody comes." He hitched up his knees, on the edge of looking annoyed again. "Except you."

"And you," Elvira said, staring back at him. Michael didn't answer; he made a noncommittal whistling noise through his teeth and looked around for a twig to chew. After he'd found one, stuck it into his mouth and chewed it for a moment, he bothered to answer. "And me," he said, giving her a cool stare.

"Do you come over here a lot?" Elvira asked. Trying to pry anything out of him was hard work.

"Pretty much," he said.

"Would it bother you if I came too?" She tried to keep the

pleading out of her voice, so he wouldn't see how important it was. Elvira pictured herself spending long afternoons, while Aunt Carrie was working at the clinic and Cousin Henry was dozing off, fixing up the drawing room for herself. Bringing over her tapestries, her ivory. Writing all her private plans and dreams in her notebook. This place fit the life she'd imagined with her father, the romantic stories she loved to read about manor houses in England. To find her own name here, to find that another Elvira had lived in this very place inspired her. She would sit in that room and write down the story of that first Elvira as it came alive in her head. She knew it would.

"Depends," Michael said slowly.

"On what?"

"Can you keep your mouth shut?" he asked. "Not mention to Carrie or anybody else about coming over here? Never say you've seen me here?"

"Well, of course!" Elvira said. "What did you think?"

"If you say anything, they'll never let you come over here. Posted. You saw the sign. Dangerous. If some old board splits and you break your neck, you could sue. The owner tries to keep people out. Carrie'd never let you hang around over here."

"I don't have to tell them every step I take," Elvira said. "And it's not my business to tell anybody where you are."

"Well, OK," Michael said. "As long as that's the way you see it." His eyes wandered to her paper sack.

"My lunch!" Elvira laughed. "I forgot to eat it. You want to split it?"

"Sure, if you've got extra."

Elvira unpacked the bag and spread out the food. He gobbled

51

up a piece of chicken and half a ham sandwich before she'd taken a bite. Elvira barely ate anything; she was too excited to be hungry, and kept looking at the inscription beside her and glancing up at the house.

By the time they finished eating and walked back through the garden, Elvira realized she'd have to hurry to get back to Carrie's. It would ruin everything if they thought she'd gotten lost and came looking for her. Elvira called the dogs from under the shade of the back porch and turned to Michael.

"Maybe I'll see you Wednesday when I come back," she said.

"Maybe," he replied. "Thanks for the lunch."

Elvira and the dogs trotted off toward the woods.

$$\underline{\qquad 6 \qquad}$$

"ELLIE!" AUNT Carrie gasped when she walked in the kitchen door. "I was fixing to call the sheriff. Cousin Henry is beside himself. What happened? You get lost back there? Decide to climb the mountain or what?"

"I'm sorry, Aunt Carrie. I ate so much, and I was tired. I just went to sleep, leaning up against a tree beside the creek. I'm sorry if you were worried."

"Henry! She's back!" Aunt Carrie called toward the porch. She turned to Elvira. "Well, you're safe and sound, honey. That's all that's important." Aunt Carrie was standing beside the sink, washing snap beans for supper. She narrowed her eyes a minute, thinking. "See anybody back in the woods? Any sign of that boy you saw yesterday, Michael Andrews?"

"That boy's run off!" Ellen Rose announced excitedly as she burst through the door.

"We brought Ellen Rose back for supper, Ellie," Aunt Carrie said. "I was so anxious and all, I forgot to mention it."

"I declare, he's nothing but trouble. With a capital T," said Ellen Rose. "That's what my daddy says and I've got to say he's right."

"What's he done so awful?" Elvira asked.

"You girls get out the ice and fix us some tea, would you?" Aunt Carrie interrupted. "I'm going to have supper on the table in about half an hour. Go and ask Cousin Henry if he'd like a little sherry, would you, Ellie? He's resting out on the porch. That clinic always tires him out."

"Why is everybody so down on that Michael boy?" Elvira whispered to Ellen Rose on the way to the porch.

"How come you're so interested?" Ellen Rose narrowed her green eyes. "Were you out there, lurking around the bushes with that boy?"

"Don't be silly!" Elvira decided not to ask any more questions about Michael—they'd just get suspicious.

"Mashed potatoes, Henry? Another piece of fish, Elvira?"

"Everything is so delicious, Aunt Carrie. You are a marvelous cook," Ellen Rose said, pushing the carrots around on her plate.

"Adequate." Aunt Carrie glanced over at her. "You don't have to eat those carrots if you don't like them."

Elvira smiled. "The fish is awfully good." It really was.

"Gorton's," Aunt Carrie said. "Have some more." She put a piece on Elvira's plate. "Food just never got my attention the way it does some people's," she said, explaining, not apologizing, to Elvira. "Never went in for making radish roses and

54

squirting mashed-potato scallops over the roast beef like that cooking lady on the TV."

"Nobody around here malnourished, as far as I can see," Cousin Henry said. "What's your opinion, Elvira?" His blue eyes were warm.

"There has to be more to life than eating," she told him, smiling. "I don't want to spend my time passing around recipes for Jell-O salad." She was thinking of some of the ladies from the party yesterday—the two that had been clucking their tongues over Laureen.

"Life is full of possibilities for you ladies," Cousin Henry said. "No reason to shut off any of them. What *do* you plan to do?"

"It seems to me we were put here to help others," Ellen Rose said. "I really admire somebody like Cousin Martha Ann, spending her life among the afflicted." She took a big swallow of milk.

"What do you plan to do yourself, Ellen Rose?" Cousin Henry asked. "Are you going to be a nurse over at the County Home too?"

"An airline stewardess," Ellen Rose said, "that's what I'm hoping for." She licked at her milk moustache. "A friend of mine's sister went off to school in Boston and got to be an airline stewardess."

"Who're you helping that way?" asked Elvira.

"You learn a lot about rescuing people and all." Ellen Rose glared at her. "If there's trouble or anything. And you get to meet lots of interesting people."

"What about you, Elvira?" Cousin Henry said. "What plans do you have?"

55

Elvira started to say she was going to be a writer, but she didn't. "I want to find my father," she blurted out, "and see what he's doing. Laureen says I'm like him."

"Wayland?" Cousin Henry looked startled. "Find Wayland? Well, that's a tall order. The court didn't have much luck when he quit helping Laureen along, as I remember." He stopped suddenly and looked embarrassed.

"Hush, Henry," said Carrie. "That's natural, Elvira. Certainly makes sense that you'd want to see your father. In fact, I can help you out a little there." She put her napkin by her plate. "Laureen's high school annual is upstairs somewhere, with Wayland's picture in it. He was big on the football team, voted most this and most that. You ever see pictures of him from back then?"

"Laureen didn't have any pictures of him at all," Elvira said, her heart beating fast. "She told me she threw them all away." She blushed. She hadn't meant to let that out.

"Well, didn't he just run off and leave you-all?" asked Ellen Rose. "That's what my daddy said. Wayland Judson just walked out the door one day and took off. Out there free as a bird with you here a burden to Aunt Carrie."

"Elvira is no burden to anybody, I can assure you," snapped Aunt Carrie, staring Ellen Rose down.

"I didn't mean it like that," Ellen Rose stammered. "I didn't mean it was her fault or anything. I mean, what else can she do? Her mother running off like that and her father vanishing into thin air."

"Laureen told you you took after Wayland, eh?" Cousin Henry said. "Well, he was dark, that's true. And Carrie is right—he was a very popular boy back in those days—a good-

looking boy. But I'll tell you who you take after—no question."
Henry's hand trembled as he drew a kitchen match out of the
box to light his pipe. "Your great-grandmother, Carrie's mother.
I saw it as soon as you walked in this door." He was having
trouble getting the pipe started. "Nobody can tell me you're not
the image of Isabelle, come back to us."

Ellen Rose's green eyes gleamed. "Now, Henry," Aunt Carrie
said, "don't excite yourself so. Elvira is nobody come back. She
is herself. We'd all best remember that." She looked at Elvira,
pursing her lips. "But if you want to see what Wayland was like,
I'll find you those old pictures. You girls give me a hand with
these dishes, and we'll go right up and look, after the kitchen's
clean."

Clearing the table, Elvira only half-listened to the conversation around her. The thought of seeing a picture of Wayland
made her heart beat fast and her hands get cold. She almost
dropped a dish.

"Careful there, honey," Aunt Carrie said, reaching for it. "All
that napping off in the woods left you kind of washed out. That
can happen." She patted Elvira on the shoulder.

"It's a shame the way families today seem to be falling
apart," Ellen Rose said, frowning at Carrie's affectionate ges-
ture. "Parents deserting their children, children deserting their
parents. My daddy says he's never seen anything like it." She
picked up a dish towel. "Where do you suppose that Michael
Andrews went to?"

"Oh, most likely he'll come back," Carrie said. "Boys will do
that once in a while."

"He just walked away from a good Christian home. You can
see people leaving if they aren't treated right, but Mamma said

57

she ran into his mother downtown today and she's all cut up. Broke down right there on Main Street."

"What's his family like?" Elvira asked, forgetting for the moment about Wayland and the picture. "Do you know them?"

"They used to have problems in the past, I heard," Ellen Rose said. "Drinking and all. The irony is, my mamma says, that he didn't leave then. He waited until his parents got themselves together to provide a real home, and then he just turned his back on it. My daddy says people are just perverse sometimes. I think he's right."

Elvira had never heard anybody quote their parents as much as Ellen Rose. She wondered if she was doing it to be mean or to impress Aunt Carrie with how adult she was. Probably both.

"Well, you can't say what somebody else's life is like," Aunt Carrie said. "From the outside, things look different."

"That's so." Ellen Rose wiped the lint off a glass. "I guess you're right, Aunt Carrie. Elvira," she said, a different tone creeping into her voice, "what was it like living in Chicago? What did you and your friends do? What kind of stores do they have there?"

Elvira smiled. Ellen Rose was giving herself away. "I don't know, Ellen Rose. Just the usual things, I guess. We didn't do much. What kind of stores? They've got lots of stores in Chicago."

"In downtown Richmond, Thalhimer's used to have a perfume fountain. I remember going there when I was a little girl and thinking there couldn't be anything more elegant in the world than that perfume fountain." Ellen Rose laughed. "I used to stick my hands in it and splash myself all over. Mamma said she couldn't come within three feet of me. I just reeked." She picked up a dry dish towel. "I love cities," she said, sighing. "The excitement and all."

Elvira found herself almost liking Ellen Rose. Then she remembered her talk at dinner and the door she'd banged yesterday. "It's a shame you haven't traveled more," she said. "Been stuck off here all your life." Aunt Carrie looked at her. "Not that it isn't very nice here," Elvira added hastily. "The woods and all."

Aunt Carrie laughed. "Never you mind, honey," she said. "I know it takes some getting used to. Bound to be a while before you feel at home here." She looked around, checking to see that everything was in order. "You're tired, Ellie. Why don't I find you that old high school book of Laureen's and you can look through it while I'm driving Ellen Rose home? I'll look in on you when I get back."

Elvira felt grateful. Nobody would be there while she looked at her father's face for the first time. "Thank you," she said. "That would be nice."

Lying in bed, turning the pages of the yearbook, Elvira put off looking for the right picture. The senior class photographs were in alphabetical order. All the boys had on suits and ties and looked serious, except for the two or three she could see right away must have been the class clowns.

Judson, Wayland. There he was. Dark, heavier than the surgeon father she'd pictured, but handsome. A square face with heavy eyebrows and a full mouth. Thick, black hair. Elvira stared. Somehow this person didn't seem real, wasn't her father in the way the other man, the one she'd imagined, was. Of course, this picture was taken when Wayland was hardly more

59

than a boy. By now, he'd be thinner, more distinguished looking.

She added graying sideburns to the face, thinned it down a little, held the book off at a distance and tried to see the photograph with kind little lines around the eyes and a pipe in the mouth. It was remarkable. The man started to look familiar. She sighed with relief. She'd had a terrible thought. "Duane," she muttered, feeling a small shock. For one awful minute, she'd thought her father looked something like Duane. Those bushy brows were probably what did it, and the jowly look a lot of teen-aged boys have. There wasn't a scrap of resemblance once she looked closely and added some detail.

Elvira flipped through the book, looking for other pictures of him and Laureen. In one photo, Laureen looked like the prom queen from an old Elvis Presley movie, her hair all teased and sprayed. Another picture showed her standing with Wayland under an arch of paper flowers; she had on a long dress with a huge, ruffled skirt, and he wore a white dinner jacket. "Sweethearts forever," it said under the picture. Elvira stared at it for a long time. Neither of them looked real.

"What do you think, honey?" Aunt Carrie came in and sat on the bed. "Strange way to meet your father. But life doesn't always do things the most sensible way." She picked at the bedspread. "Don't let that talk about Wayland—from Henry and Ellen Rose—get you down. Everybody has his strong points, and his reasons for doing what he does."

"He just couldn't get along with Laureen, I guess," Elvira said. "And maybe he wanted to do something in the world. Probably that's why he left when he did."

"You may be right. He got himself tied down before he meant

to. I'm glad you don't resent that so much you can't look for the good in him, Elvira. Let the past be the past, I say."

"Yes, Aunt Carrie," Elvira said carefully. Elvira wanted Aunt Carrie to know she felt a strong tie to her father. If things worked out, and they went off together, she didn't want Aunt Carrie to be hurt. "Like you always say, family is who you are. Laureen was all the time saying I was like him."

"Laureen ought to have told you more than that," Aunt Carrie said. "And she ought to have saved some pictures to show you."

"She kept pictures of everybody else." Elvira wanted to ask what had happened between her parents, but some little voice inside warned her not to. She *knew* about her father, didn't she? Tonight she'd found out that he looked just the way she had thought he would. That must mean that the other ideas she'd had about him were real too. Snooping into the past might not be fair to him.

"Well, honey, you've got to remember she got her feelings hurt pretty bad. He shouldn't have gone off and left Laureen flat. He should have helped her with raising you. Paid some of the expenses. It is hard to take on all that responsibility all alone. And Laureen was just a girl."

"Maybe something happened to him?" Elvira knew better than to bring up her amnesia idea. If she said that out loud, it would sound ridiculous.

Aunt Carrie looked at her hard, a little startled. "As far as I know, he's all right, honey. I never heard that he'd had an accident or anything. I think your first idea is the right one. He was too young to face up to family life."

"Maybe Laureen did something that drove him away," Elvira

61

suggested. "I get the feeling she feels guilty about the whole thing." Her mother was probably as selfish then as she was today.

Carrie looked uncomfortable. "Well, I don't know, honey. I don't think you should be too hard on your mother." She fidgeted with the bedspread, rubbing it between her fingers. "Look at it this way, Elvira," she said finally. "When Wayland left, Laureen's pride was hurt. You know Laureen is supersensitive that way. Has to hold her head higher than the rest."

Elvira nodded.

"I think she didn't want to be reminded. Was afraid people were saying she couldn't hold on to her husband. Not that they would," Aunt Carrie said hastily, "but that's the kind of thing Laureen would worry over. Pride is what keeps her from coming back here, don't you think? And what told her to throw away those pictures?"

"And not having gotten to be an actress, too. Being a waitress still. That would make coming back hard." Elvira understood that side of her mother well enough. Proud. Surprised, Elvira suddenly saw a resemblance between herself and Laureen. It made her uncomfortable, and she fell silent.

"You be glad about who you are, Elvira," Aunt Carrie said. "That's the important thing. And you respect your parents, too. That's right. Nobody in this world goes through life without making a mistake now and then. You look for the good—that's what I try to do." Carrie straightened the fold of the spread at the foot of Elvira's bed. "My parents died when I was young. Maybe that's why having family like you is so important to me." She looked down at the floor.

"What happened to them?" Elvira tried to imagine Aunt

Carrie a child. What she saw was a sixty-three-year-old lady in a print apron, only much smaller.

"An accident, that's all," Aunt Carrie said. "Both killed when I was a girl. At the same time."

"How awful," Elvira said. "I'm sorry. How did it happen?"

"I'll tell you about it some other time." Aunt Carrie smoothed down her skirt as if she were pushing memories away, getting herself in order. "Now that you're here, we'll have plenty of time for talking. No need to blurt everything out right away. You get some sleep now." She leaned forward and kissed Elvira on the forehead. "Sleep tight."

Elvira lay back in bed and thought about Carrie's parents. How sad that both had died at once. Probably it had been a car wreck, or a train accident or something. And Aunt Carrie was such a kind person, one of the kindest Elvira had ever met.

Elvira didn't think about Aunt Carrie for long. Her mind kept turning back to that old house where she'd seen her name on the gravestone.

She found herself thinking about Michael, too. That afternoon, jutting out his chin, wagging that stalk of grass in his teeth, he had seemed sort of tiresome. But now, knowing he had run away from home, that he must be living at that place all by himself, he began to seem much more romantic.

"Very masculine," Elvira muttered, remembering the way he had clenched his jaw and stared at her. The way he'd hardly talked at all. "Strong. I should have seen that." Just as she had held Wayland's picture off at arm's length to see it right, she squared Michael's shoulders, smoothed down his cowlick and realized that he was a very attractive boy.

Elvira imagined herself back at the plantation house, smelling again that bitter scent of boxwood in the sun. A gray figure, like a misty flame, shivered down the back steps and floated over the old brick walks toward her. Elvira wasn't afraid. She wanted to meet her, the other Elvira.

All the talk she had listened to that day whirled in her head. Wayland's photograph blended with images of the old house as Elvira drew nearer sleep. She, Michael and her father, wearing the white dinner jacket he had on in the picture, were together in the house. The boxwood was clipped and the garden was full of roses. She saw herself on the winding brick path, standing beside her father. He was a mixture of the man she had always seen and the boy in the yearbook. Still tall and distinguished, but now he had bushier eyebrows and more wave in his hair.

They were having dinner in the tall-ceilinged dining room. Her father was carving the turkey. A white linen cloth covered the table. Silver gleamed and crystal rang like a bell.

"Why don't you get married in the garden, by the white rosebush?" her father suggested, raising his glass.

Then suddenly she was on the porch, watching expectantly for something. An Elvira made of mist, gray and luminous, came floating. She stretched out a hand, gentle as a butterfly, toward her. It was herself meeting herself.

"Home, Elvira," the mist girl said. "You came home."

With the morning sun streaming through her window, Elvira still felt the peace of that odd new feeling of being where she belonged. She sat up slowly and swung her feet down to rest lightly on the rag rug. White feet like lilies. Everything seemed brushed by magic.

It would be so perfect—she, her father and Michael all together in the house in the woods. He could come back, Elvira thought, as she dressed. He could buy the house and they could all fix it up. Michael could stay with them.

And after she grew up and became a writer, she could live there. And her father could spend vacations. If she and Michael did get married, it would be ideal, unless he wanted to travel or something.

Elvira crawled under the bed, fishing out her shoes. It was all pretty silly, she told herself, tying the laces. But it wasn't completely impossible.

7

"I SHOULD have had her out here Sunday," Aunt Carrie said, sliding an egg onto Elvira's plate. "I apologize, honey. My thoughts just didn't go past this family. Selfish to want to keep you all to ourselves."

"My father's sister?" Toast stuck in Elvira's throat; it was impossible to swallow. "My Aunt Joyce? I never knew he had a sister!"

"I know. It's a disgrace the way all ties were cut there. Until you mentioned it at supper last night, I hadn't given Wayland's family a thought myself." She turned to Henry, who had just rolled himself into the kitchen in his wheelchair.

"I was just telling Elvira about her Aunt Joyce, Henry— Wayland's sister. We forgot all about her when we were talking about who she'd want to meet."

"Joyce Judson?" Henry said, not sounding pleased. "Why seek her out?"

"Joyce Arliss she is now. Married Lamont Arliss not long after Laureen left. And it's natural Elvira might want to see her, have some contact with that side of her family."

"Humph." Cousin Henry wheeled himself up to the table. "Let sleeping dogs lie, I always say. Let this lovely child find her family right here where she belongs, with us." He reached over and patted Elvira on the hand.

"My aunt still lives in Charlottesville?" Elvira moved her hand away from Cousin Henry, smiling at him politely. He was sweet to care, but it wasn't fair to hold her back from the chance to find her father, to move into the life she'd always wanted. "Couldn't you call her up, Aunt Carrie?" she asked, her voice quavering. "Maybe I could go by and see her? Get to know her?"

Aunt Carrie looked doubtful for a minute; she glanced at Cousin Henry and frowned. After a pause, she said, "Sure I can, honey, if that's what you want. But don't get your hopes up sky-high. Don't get to thinking that seeing Joyce is going to mean seeing Wayland. I don't know how much they keep up with each other. It's been years since I've seen Joyce except for running into her downtown or something."

Henry frowned. "Are you sure you know what you're doing there, Carrie? Getting our Elvira mixed in with those Judsons might just be too much family all at once."

Elvira gulped a little milk. "I'd *like* to meet her, though, Cousin Henry. Really. It's important. Could I see her soon, Aunt Carrie, do you think?"

"Well, if that's what you want, there's no time like the present," Aunt Carrie said. "Excuse me. I'll go call her." She went to the hall to telephone.

Elvira finished her egg. Already she was picturing this new aunt—her father's sister. She would have some of his distinguished look, a woman's version of it, of course. She would be tall, and her dark hair would be streaked with gray, like Wayland's. Sort of a ballet-dancer-looking lady—graceful and reserved, but friendly and warm when you got to know her. His sister. Elvira couldn't believe it. It made her dream into an omen. She heard Carrie talking; it was all working out.

"Did she know I was here?" she asked, when Carrie came back.

"No, honey," Carrie answered. "She was real surprised to hear it. But she was pleased," she added quickly, "real pleased and excited about meeting you. Said it was like those people you read about in the newspaper once in a while—finding long-lost relatives." Aunt Carrie took a bite of toast and frowned. "But, Elvira, don't get too carried away, hear? Don't expect Joyce to seem like family right off. Anymore than we did, sweetie." She fiddled with her spoon. "It takes a while to get the feel of people—to feel kin to them."

"And I still say it's too much too soon," Henry boomed out, gesturing with toast and jam. "I still say let the girl get used to one set of relatives at a time. Enough is enough." He reached over and patted Elvira again.

Cousin Henry was afraid she'd go off with her father, Elvira thought. That was why he was talking against her visiting her aunt. He probably sensed, just the way she did, that her father's people were the ones Elvira belonged with. Aunt Carrie and Cousin Henry were sweet and decent, Elvira thought a little guiltily. But they couldn't keep her from her *real* family.

"Friday, Joyce and I said," Aunt Carrie went on. "When I go

to the clinic, I'll drop you off at Joyce's for a get-acquainted visit. I'm just working two hours Friday—it's the short afternoon. But that ought to be just about right, give you time to get to know each other a little."

"Thanks so much for calling her, Aunt Carrie," Elvira said, finishing her breakfast. "It was nice of you."

"Not at all, Elvira. I should have let her know as soon as I heard you were coming. We can't keep you all to ourselves." Carrie aimed that remark at Henry, who rustled his newspaper angrily but made no reply. "Come on, Ellie, let's get the dishes done. Can't waste time the whole day sitting here chatting, can we?"

Elvira smiled and collected the plates. She swished her hands through the suds dreamily, imagining Friday. Almost as exciting was the thought of going to the house on Wednesday to tell Michael.

Thinking of the house, Elvira remembered how free and alive she'd felt, walking through those empty rooms. Then finding her name. And feeling the way she did about Michael. And the dream. And now her aunt. It was all leading somewhere. Taking her to her real family. Elvira felt as if her dream had never stopped, as if she were still in it.

Wednesday, she almost ran through the woods in her haste to get to the house. Carrying one of her tapestries and her lunch sack, she had to slow down once to adjust her packages, and again to disentangle her jeans when they caught on a blackberry vine. These small delays couldn't dim her feeling that a kind of magic was working in her life now, a fate that was finally arranging things into a pattern she'd foreseen herself.

Michael came around the house just as she crossed the field near the boxwood bushes. "You're back," he said. Beads of sweat lined his upper lip, and a cowlick jutted up beside his part. Standing there with his hands on his hips, he didn't look a bit like the boy in the rose garden in her dream. For a split second Elvira almost panicked. Then she looked up at the house and her certainty came back. From what Ellen Rose had said, and from her dream, Elvira knew she had seen inside to the real Michael.

"Hi," she said, suddenly shy.

"You didn't talk," he said. "I thought you might, but you didn't."

"How do you know?"

"*Because*, if you had, somebody would have come snooping around, looking for me. I watched to make sure, but nobody has."

"I *told* you I wouldn't tell." She was annoyed.

"Yeah, but you never know." He turned and jumped three long, feet-together jumps to the front steps. He sat down, yawning.

Elvira walked over hastily and sat down beside him. "I heard you ran away. Everybody's talking about it!"

"Yeah?" he said. "Fire up."

"Well, it is kind of exciting." Elvira leaned forward, elbows on her knees. "Living out here all alone and all."

"Sure," he said. "Thrilling. I get to listen to the squirrels yammering, and if I'm lucky I might spend an afternoon grinning back at some old possum. Exciting."

"Well, why did you come, if you didn't want to?"

"Didn't have no choice."

"What do you mean?"

"Guess."

"Your parents?" Sympathy lowered Elvira's voice.

"Saved," Michael snorted. He leaned back on the steps, clasping his hands behind his head. "Went out to that tabernacle place and got saved. My mom did, anyway. And Dad was right behind her, like always."

"They're real religious?" Elvira was puzzled.

"You better believe it," Michael snapped. "And leaving nobody else a minute's peace ever since they got sucked in. Hounding me and picking at me and praying over me."

"I guess that would get on your nerves."

"Private, I can swallow it," he said, sitting up abruptly, his eyes bright with indignation. "Private, all that praying and ranting, I can stomach. To each his own, I say." He fished around in the grass by the step for something to chew. "*Public*, that's something else. That was two steps past what I am set up to endure, that's all."

"What do you mean," Elvira asked, "public?"

"Just precisely *that* is what I mean. Prayed over. Testified about. In public. Out loud. Getting up on Sunday morning and calling on the Lord to rescue me, her son. Calling me a sinner. Getting personal about my sins. Ranting on and turning me into some kind of example. Jeeesus!" Michael was pale and still, staring into the boxwood bush.

"And you had to sit there and listen?" Elvira turned red, imagining herself sitting innocently in a pew, suddenly being made into a spectacle.

71

"Not me!" Michael spat. "You won't catch me inside that place!"

"How did you know about it, then?"

"Dawn Marie Wilson, that's how," Michael said, making a face. "Called me on the telephone. Didn't give herself time to get out of her church clothes or nothing. Just must have rushed right home to call me and make my day. Probably called half the junior class before Sunday dinner. Wouldn't want anybody to miss out."

"That's why you left?" Elvira asked.

"Wouldn't you?" he asked in a strangled voice. "Could you stand it?"

"Well, I don't know." Elvira tried to see both sides of the situation. "It would be embarrassing," she admitted after a moment.

"*Embarrassing?*" he snorted. "Try and feature me going back to school after that. Half those snots got no use for me as it is, all the trouble my dad used to get into back when they were drinking. I carried that burden all those years. Now this. I have to be able to look at myself in the mirror!"

Elvira looked at his white face, the freckles standing out sharply, and in the pit of her stomach felt just what he was feeling. "That social worker—Mrs. Macy!" she blurted out, falling over her words.

"What?" he asked, startled.

"The same thing happened to me! When Laureen, my mother, left, they sent over a caseworker. She wrote up notes, made me into a case. Public, like you say."

His eyes widened. "No kidding?" he said. "A caseworker?"

For the first time since they'd met, his face unfroze and he looked straight at her without squinting, or tilting his chin, or waggling grass, or spitting.

"But it isn't going to matter much longer. I am about to go to see my father's sister—get back in touch with that side of my family."

"What'll that do?"

"I'm like my father. My mother was always telling me that," Elvira said. Some tightness inside her had relaxed. It all came rushing out. "It's just that I've always felt out of place somehow. As if everybody else knew how they connected to things and I didn't. I've always felt like an orphan people were taking in. Even when I lived with Laureen." She frowned, trying to get her thoughts straight. "But everybody comes from somewhere—has a connection to something."

"Connections aren't necessarily all that great," Michael said. "People pulling and yanking at you to do this and that."

Elvira was too far inside her thoughts now to notice him. "As soon as I saw this house and went inside, all the feelings I had about my real family, where I really belonged, came clear."

Michael leaned back on his elbows. "You've got the right to dream if you want to," he said, "think about how you'd like things to be."

"This *isn't* just a dream. I told you—all my life Laureen has been telling me how I'm like my father. 'Two peas in a pod,' she used to say. That means something. I didn't make it up."

"Nobody said you did. Take it easy."

"And now my Aunt Joyce. Day after tomorrow, seeing her. There's a kind of plan behind it all—don't you see? Things

73

worked together in a mysterious way and brought me here," Elvira insisted. "I never saw anything or anybody with my name before. You have to admit it's an unusual name. And here I am brought to the place where it came from. And now, starting to find my father." She paused, out of breath.

Michael looked at her without comment. Then he said, "You want a father? Take mine. You're welcome." And he got that frozen look again. Elvira felt guilty. She'd been selfish, raving on about herself.

"What are *you* planning to do, Michael? You can't live out here all by yourself for good."

He snorted. "Hardly. No, I'm just here getting my plans firmed up. Waiting for a deal to come through. A kid to pay me for my bike. He's got to raise some cash. I figure to go west. Back where you came from. Moline, Illinois. My brother lives there. He's married."

"That's why you were asking me about the bus and all," Elvira said.

"That's right, you've got it." He broke off a twig from the bush and started peeling it. "But now, I'm figuring to hitch. That's my latest plan."

"Does he know you're coming?"

"Naw, how could he? But last Christmas, when he called, he said, 'Why don't you come out sometime?' He's my brother, for Christ's sake—he's going to have to be glad to see me. I figure I'll hang around with him and his wife for a couple of weeks. Maybe he'll help me find a job, get set on my own."

"Are you old enough to do that?"

"I can take care of myself," Michael said. "Watch. I been working for years already. Saved up two hundred dollars once.

Got seventy-five now, even without the bike money." He looked across at her coolly.

"Really? That's great. What did you do?"

"Different things. Bag-boy jobs, filling station. Couple of years ago, when he lived in town, I worked for your Cousin Henry. Yard work, that sort of stuff."

Elvira remembered how Henry had raved on about "that scamp" when Michael had come past on his bike, and how Aunt Carrie changed the subject when anybody talked about him. "Michael," she asked, "what happened there? Why do they get so jumpy about you—Aunt Carrie and Cousin Henry?"

Michael looked away. "They have reasons," he said.

"What kind? They tiptoe around your name as if you were some poisonous snake. Cousin Henry raves on about calling the sheriff when you ride past."

"He has reasons."

"*What* reasons?"

"I listened in on them once. Your Cousin Henry was getting sicker and having trouble by himself, and one day your Aunt Carrie came and talked to him about going out and living with her. I was supposed to be working out in the yard and I came in to get a drink of water and I stayed in the kitchen and listened to them. To their private talk." Michael turned red. "It was a lousy thing to do."

"Well, big deal." Elvira snorted. "You'd think you tried to burn down their house or something. And how earthshaking could their secrets be, anyway?" She sat back on her heels and looked thoughtful. "Maybe that's just it. Suppose you were somebody who never has anything romantic or exciting happen in your life. You just sit in one small place and cut the grass and drink lemonade. Then you get so you get excited over nothing. You think some minuscule thing is super fascinating and important."

Michael was silent. Like Henry and Carrie, he just didn't seem to want to talk about it. Elvira felt disgusted. Aunt Carrie and Cousin Henry were nice, but, just as Laureen had said, living off in the woods the way they did they spent their time making mountains out of molehills.

Michael looked up at the sky suddenly. Acorns were bouncing off the porch roof; the wind was rising. They had been so intent on their conversation that they hadn't noticed the clouds gathering. "I got to get my stuff out of the woods. I moved it there after you came, to make sure you didn't send anybody after me." He looked apologetic. "I didn't know you so good then. If I don't get my sleeping bag back into the summer kitchen, it'll get soaked."

"I was going to fix up the drawing room some. I brought a pen and my notebook for writing. I think I'll go inside and sit and write about the first Elvira. Unless you want me to help."

"Naw," Michael said. "You go on in. I'll see you later." He ran off toward the back garden.

Elvira walked up the porch steps and went inside the house. Shadows had closed in, making the house dark. It felt hushed and expectant, with an electric, before-a-storm feeling. Elvira shivered, imagining suddenly that she might see the pale figure float around the doorframe and reach out for her with ghost fingers. She told herself to calm down and went into the drawing room. It was lighter in there than in the hall, and the elegance of the room, with its tall windows and fireplace, its remnants of pale paper clinging to the walls, made her feel sad, sad for the people who had lived here.

It was just the mood she needed to write her story. Elvira spread the Indian cotton square in the corner opposite the fireplace and sat down, leaning back against the wall. Then she opened her notebook and began to write the story of the other Elvira as it came into her mind.

8

THE TRAGEDY OF ELVIRA MATTHEWS

Elvira Matthews was a slender girl with skin the color of lilies and eyes like violet pools. Ebony hair swirled around her fine-boned face, sometimes pulled back above her shell-like ears. Her mother having died in childbirth, the young girl had lived all her life with her handsome father. He was a distinguished man, his black hair touched with silver in places, his sideburns and eyebrows gray and aristocratic-looking.

Elvira looked around the room. The rain was washing the windowpanes now, blowing in places where the glass was broken.

The girl and her father lived in a plantation house in the woods. Evenings they sat in their drawing room together, the candlelight making the numerous silver vases and bowls shimmer around them. Their devotion for each other was beautiful to see. At balls, Elvira always danced first with her father.

Living the life of a typical southern girl, Elvira never expected her life to be shattered by war. But when the Civil War came, her life changed.

The storm was now directly overhead. When lightning lit up the room for an instant, Elvira thought of the war and of musket fire and cannon booming and people running and the smell of smoke. She needed every bit of ability to make this part of the story right. She turned to the front of her notebook, where she kept her list of phrases. Whenever she read a striking phrase, Elvira would get out her notebook and enter it. She had several pages of them.

In the face of the war, Elvira felt the tearing of an anguish more profound than any grief she had yet experienced. A sense of powerful foreboding, as if some awful fate were in store for her, almost overcame the delicate girl. A dark shadow seemed to swoop down over her eyes, and she almost swooned when she first heard that her father would be riding off. Ashamed, she quickly reminded herself that it was her duty to send her father off bravely, never suspecting the depth of despair that his daughter was concealing behind her carefree exterior. Lithe and handsome, her father strode off in his well-cut gray uniform, his face hard and masculine at the thought of defending all that he held dear.

Shortly after her father's departure, a boy she had

known since childhood suddenly told her he loved her. Holding her in his firm arms, he pressed kisses on her eyelids.

"Charles," Elvira gasped, drawing away, "I will not lie to you. I have always regarded you in the light of a brother. As such, you will always be dear to me."

The young officer groaned. "Give me a reason to live, Elvira! Say you will be my wife!"

Her heart pounded and her head whirled. "All right, Charles," she whispered finally. "When you come back, I will be yours." She gave him a bunch of violets from her waist. Captain Charles Paxton fastened them in his hat and rode away.

Elvira saw it all before her, the dark-haired Charles in his gray uniform begging and pleading before the marble mantel. Candlelight making the polished wood of the furniture glow. Elvira stretched and thought, listening to the rain. Maybe she could use another character to round out the story better.

Always protected and cherished, Elvira now found herself alone. All her life her father had hovered protectively over her. Nothing was ever too good for his much-adored, slender young daughter. But alone as she was, Elvira was quick to help another less fortunate than herself.

Down the road, in a shacky home with a tin roof and tarpaper sides, was a sad case. A daughter, Eleanora Rose, had been deserted by her parents—a scraggly man who chewed tobacco and a shiftless woman who never wore shoes. The two had stolen off during the night without a thought for the daughter they left behind. The girl had none of Elvira's courage. Instead of taking up her life, as Elvira had done, she squawked like a stuck chicken and complained to all the neighbors. Elvira immediately invited the girl to her plantation. Eleanora couldn't believe her good fortune and stared around her, gawking at the luxurious appointments of the handsome house.

Loneliness was a constant companion to the girl who had taken onto her slender frame the responsibilities for running a gigantic plantation and overseeing the needs of the scatterbrained Eleanora Rose. One afternoon, as purple shadows closed in around the frilled green leaves interwoven together in the back garden, Elvira sat at her window almost blind to the beauty of the scene, so great was her despair.

Under the trees at the end of the garden, something blue moved. Elvira's long white hand flew to her throat. Was a Yankee soldier lurking in the forest?

Calling Eleanora Rose, Elvira set off down the path. Little did she suspect that, overcome with foreboding at the thought of finding her worst enemy, she would instead find true love, tragically. Eleanora hung back, her legs shaking under her long skirt.

Elvira read over what she had done. It did sound like those romances Laureen got from her club every month, she thought proudly. It really did.

A hand in a blue sleeve protruded from behind a tree. A wounded Yankee soldier was lying right at the feet of Elvira and Eleanora Rose. "Ahhhhhhhh!" The yellow-haired

Eleanora screeched like a scalded cat. Calmly Elvira beckoned, summoning the quaking Eleanora to her side. "You are hurt," she said, pity moving her at the sight of his suffering. "We must help you."

Captain Michael Judson was a handsome man, fair and well muscled. His blue eyes gleamed like hard steel. His nostrils had a powerful, masculine flare even in his weakened state.

Elvira frowned. He sounded sort of like a horse. She *knew* she'd seen that nostril detail dozens of times. It *had* to be OK.

The two girls placed him on a sofa in the drawing room. For days he lay between life and death.

As his strength returned, Elvira found herself in a torrential whirlpool of raging emotion. Looking through her lashes at Michael Judson on her drawing room sofa, Elvira experienced a wild fire in her bloodstream. Unexpected shivers took hold of her spine. She told herself that she was promised to Charles, that this man was the enemy. But Charles was merely a boy. Michael was a man. Did he suspect the nature of the feelings which he had awakened in her woman's heart?

Suddenly one afternoon Elvira found herself in his arms, feeling the rough wool of his sleeve against her cheek. Then his lips were pressed to hers, urgent and demanding. This was far different from the sisterly affection she felt for Charles. Michael grew stronger every day, and as he did, Elvira felt joy at his recovery, but despair at the knowledge he must soon leave.

82

When that day came, Michael bade her farewell, whispering that soon, soon, he would be back.

Elvira watched him until he disappeared under the giant oaks. Then she sank, semiconscious, to the sofa. After a time, aroused by the sounds of dogs barking, Elvira rushed, heart leaping, to the porch.

By fatal chance, there stood Captain Charles, home on leave this very day. *Just twenty minutes earlier,* Elvira thought, horrified, *and who knows what might have happened?*

Her relief was to be short-lived.

"Guess what, Elvira?" asked Captain Charles.

"Doesn't sound quite right," Elvira muttered, and wrote "RW," for *rewrite,* next to it.

"You are safe nowhere in this day and age. On this very road I met a Yankee officer." Elvira turned to ice. "One less Yankee murdering our men. I brought you a souvenir, my love." He held out to her—a sword.

Trembling, Elvira looked at the name engraved on the handle. MICHAEL JUDSON.

Elvira fell forward in a faint. She hung between life and death, suffering from brain fever. Eleanora Rose, Charles and Elvira's father, summoned home, stood about the bed, sobbing. The only kindness Eleanora Rose had known had come from this slender girl whose life now hung by a thread. The skinny girl was desolated.

Coming back to consciousness, Elvira asked to hold the sword. "Perhaps it makes her feel safe," her father said, seeing how she clutched it to her white bosom.

Imagine his distress when, one day, he found his beloved daughter, her violet eyes shut for the last time, black lashes lying like the wings of birds on her ivory cheeks, with Captain Michael's sword piercing her heart.

Elvira's inconsolable father lived only months after her death. The plantation gradually became covered by weeds and wild flowers. The only thing that ever came to disturb the peace of that garden was the slight figure of a girl with a shimmer of pearly light about her. She had long, swirling hair, dark as night, and in her hand carried a Civil War sword. As the years went by, many were moved to tears at the sight of Elvira, floating down the paths of the garden where she had spent her tragically short life.

Elvira stood up and closed her notebook. It was getting late; she would find Michael, say good-bye and head home. She went quietly out the front door. The wet grass swished around her ankles, soaking her sneakers. The storm was over.

9

IDING INTO town that Friday afternoon, Elvira was cold as ice even though heat waves were vibrating off the surface of the road. She tried to concentrate on Aunt Carrie's hand on the stick shift, as it moved up and back. Aunt Carrie chattered on, but Elvira didn't even try to answer. In a few minutes she would meet her father's sister—her Aunt Joyce.

Her aunt's house was just like all the others near it, but it was painted lavender. Red-and-white ranch houses, all with big windows in the front and carports off to the side, lined the block. Some had little rows of petunias out front; one yard had two plastic flamingos. Aunt Joyce's yard had a little sign hanging on a post: WELCOME—THE ARLISSES it said. Somebody was peering out from behind a lamp in the middle of the big picture window as they pulled up in the truck.

"You go on in, honey," Aunt Carrie said. "I'll be back in a couple of hours—give you time to get acquainted." A little awkwardly, she leaned over and hugged Elvira. Elvira quickly pushed open the door handle and jumped out.

"Come on in, precious!"

A dark-haired, fat lady in stretch pants was standing on the little entry porch, waving. She held the door open while Elvira came inside. The house was air-conditioned and dark; Elvira blinked, adjusting to the change from the glare outside. The fat lady smelled of honeysuckle toilet water.

"Wayland's girl!" The lady reached for her. Elvira drew back a step, but Joyce caught her anyway. It was like being sucked up by a sofa. The woman was encased in elastic, girdled and brassiered. Elvira pulled loose, feeling dizzy.

"Hello, Aunt Joyce," she said.

"Wayland's girl!" Joyce exclaimed again. "Let me look at you, sugar!" She held Elvira's shoulders and looked into her face. "You've got his eyes!" she crowed. "Those sexy Judson eyes. Well, let's hope they don't cause you the trouble they caused that brother of mine!" She laughed and reached for a cigarette. "That look the girls always thought was so deep and mysterious!" She sat down on the sofa and patted the place beside her. "Come sit here, so I can look at you." She lit her cigarette and took a deep breath, shutting her eyes and tilting up her chin when she exhaled.

Elvira sat on the other end of the sofa.

"When Laureen cleared out of here, telling everybody to eat her dust, we all figured that was that. I never figured to see either of you again." Joyce adjusted her white knit top; it had started to ride up, revealing a roll of flesh at her waist.

Elvira shrank into the arm of the sofa.

"Not that I blame her. Wayland didn't treat her right. He didn't. But that's all in the past, right, honey? No reason to let that cause bad blood between kin." She waited for Elvira to answer.

"No," Elvira said.

"I'm happy you feel that way, baby," Joyce said. "Very happy. I know your daddy hasn't done right by you, really. But he's not the bad person your mamma and aunt probably told you he is."

Elvira could barely speak. She felt as if she were in a bad dream. "They never said anything like that," she finally answered. "What's wrong with him?"

"Wrong with him!" Joyce threw back her head and laughed, letting her top ride up without bothering to pull it down again. "Wrong with Wayland! Nothing much. Except a terminal case of being overromantic, if you get what I mean. Very susceptible to the ladies. From the time he was in junior high, had a string of girls running after him. Used to drive Mamma up the wall. 'Ladies' men come to no good, Wayland,' she used to tell him. 'You're getting your head turned. The foundations of your life will turn to sand.' Mamma was a big Bible reader," Joyce explained. "But, of course, he never listened. Mamma nearly tore the house down. 'Mixed up with tramps and hussies of the night!' I can still hear her yelling and shrieking." Joyce ground out her cigarette. "Of course, Laureen wasn't any tramp, no matter what Mamma said. I just want you to get the picture. See why Wayland cleared out. He was getting it from both sides."

"What do you mean," Elvira asked, "both sides?"

"Well, *all* sides, really. That Wayland was the center of more consternation than we've seen around here since Appomattox. You'd better believe." She shook her head at Elvira.

"What do you mean? Who was mad at him?" Elvira was suddenly afraid to hear what Joyce was saying.

"Well, Mamma was, like I told you. For getting himself into trouble—for getting married so sudden." Joyce looked embarrassed. "And Laureen was, because she thought he was going to settle down and be a husband, once she had that piece of paper on him." Joyce chuckled and shook her head. "Probably she was just the first of a number of ladies hoping that Wayland would settle down."

Elvira's eyes widened. She remembered Aunt Carrie's telling her that Laureen felt embarrassed about "not being able to hold on to her husband," or about people's thinking that. It wasn't just because he disappeared, then. It was even before that, leaving her and running around with other women. And getting married "so sudden." Elvira knew what that meant. She felt sick. For a minute, she thought she might faint. In one horrible moment the mystery had been solved. Now she knew why her mother always acted so guilty when Elvira asked her what had happened. She knew why Aunt Carrie had acted so uncomfortable talking to her the other night. Wayland and Laureen never wanted to get married. Probably they had never even been in love. She remembered the picture in the book—"Sweethearts forever"—and shuddered. It had all been a mistake. *She* had been a mistake.

And he hadn't even had the decency to stick with Laureen for a year after the baby was born. After *she* was born, Elvira corrected herself miserably. He just went blithely on, chasing girls and ignoring his wife and baby. That was Wayland. That was her distinguished, kind and aristocratic father. Elvira reeled back against the sofa cushions, helpless to stop all these revelations pouring forth from her aunt. Joyce was never going to stop talking. "Shut up!" Elvira screamed silently, deep inside herself. "Shut up!"

"Then," Joyce went on, "there were those Peytons—Laureen's family. They always have had a high opinion of themselves, never did seem to think Wayland was good enough for Laureen. Though, if you want my opinion, they've had their share of scandals like everybody else. At least, Wayland never shot anybody." Joyce looked smug.

Elvira didn't know what Joyce was talking about, but she didn't care. All she wanted now was to live through the next hour and a half—get out of this living room and crawl off somewhere by herself. "I never heard anybody say anything bad about him," she whispered. "Aunt Carrie said some good things, really. And she never said anything about your family."

"Don't say *my* family, honey," Joyce corrected. "It's yours, too."

Elvira looked wildly around the room for a way to change the subject. "That's a pretty picture over there. Who is it?" A dark-haired girl in a satin wedding gown smiled stiffly at the camera.

"Can't you tell? Don't say I've changed *that* much, sugar. That's me, on my wedding day. Of course, by then, you and Laureen had left. Otherwise, you could have been my little flower girl. Come over and take a closer look. Then we can go out to the kitchen and have a Coke or something. A piece of cake. You look to me like you could use a little solid food. And nobody ever turned down my chocolate cake yet."

Elvira was grateful for the chance to move around. She felt so numb, she was surprised her legs worked. But they did, and she walked across the room, looked at Joyce's picture, then moved into the kitchen. She hoped nobody could tell that her mouth was dry and her head was humming.

Sitting at the dinette table, Elvira looked out the window at the sun beating down into the backyard. She saw a swing set and a wading pool.

"You have children?" she asked.

"Sure do, sweetie, and you'll get to meet them any minute. Lori Ann and Shawn Eric. They're all excited about their new cousin. I sent them over to a friend's to play—give us a chance to talk a bit. But they'll be back anytime."

"Good," Elvira said, trying to swallow her cake. If the children came, she could get away from Joyce.

"Just one thing, sugar, before they get here. I wanted to talk to you seriously a minute. I hope you weren't looking for much in the way of help from Wayland now, were you? Carrie isn't bringing you here so I'll find him and she can get a suit going or anything, is she?" Joyce frowned into her glass. "I know by all rights Wayland ought to be paying support, but I don't think he's got it. He's got another family now, a little boy, and his wife's never been well. And, between you and me, I don't know that Wayland has changed all that much, if you get what I mean. Once a skirt-chaser, always a skirt-chaser. On his death-bed, Wayland will be eyeing the nurses, mark my word." She snorted. "But I'm sure you heard all that. I know Carrie must have given you an earful, whatever you say."

"I wasn't looking for anything," Elvira said stiffly. "Nobody ever said anything about him paying money or anything. Aunt

Carrie would never do anything like that," she said, suddenly happy that what she was saying was true. "Aunt Carrie would never go around squeezing money out of people. Cousin Henry either!"

"Calm down, honey. That's fine. I just wanted to make sure. I'm glad everybody sees the way it is. Because then I can be a little more open with you. Give you a little more to go on. Can you believe Wayland was here, not six months ago? I hadn't seen him in years, myself. And now you showing up. He's in Cincinnati now, or was then. Before you know it, we'll be holding a family reunion—all us Judsons!" She threw back her head and laughed.

Elvira crumpled the paper napkin in her fist; the cake sat in her stomach like a rock. Mercifully, she heard children's voices out in the carport. The door pushed open and a little boy and girl came in, their eyes wide with curiosity.

"This Uncle Wayland's girl?" Shawn Eric asked, walking over to his mother.

"Surely is. Your cousin Elvira. You say 'Hi,' Shawn Eric."

"Hi," the little boy said, his eyes widening even more. He was wiry, with green eyes and blond hair. He wore a VIRGINIA IS FOR LOVERS T-shirt.

"Hi," Elvira said. "and hi to you too, Lori Ann."

"You talk funny," Shawn Eric said. "Like a Yankee."

"So does Uncle Wayland," Lori Ann said. "He talks Yankee, too."

"You kids are a scream," Aunt Joyce said. "Never miss a trick." She yawned. "Why don't you go out in the yard with the kids a bit, Elvira? Give you-all a chance to get acquainted."

91

"It's too hot out there," Lori Ann whined. "I don't want to go outside."

"Maybe I could push you on the swing," Elvira said. "That would cool you off."

In the yard, Elvira pushed Lori Ann, then Shawn Eric, without speaking. Numbly, she followed behind when they offered to show her the house where their friend lived. Lori Ann grabbed her hand, and she curled her fingers around the child's automatically.

"Look at that!" Joyce cooed from the back door. "Hand in hand. Cousins forever. Your Aunt Carrie is pulling up, Elvira." She held the door open and Elvira walked in.

Halfway across the living room, Joyce stopped and snapped her fingers. "About to let you go off without your surprise! Can't do that!" She picked up a snapshot that was lying on the coffee table. "Guess who? Your daddy. You keep it, I've got some others." She patted Elvira on the shoulder. "We'll see you again real soon, Elvira." She waved out the door to Carrie.

"Thank you," Elvira said haltingly. "Thank you." She went out to the curb, clutching the snapshot.

Out on the street she stopped, held it up and looked at the man who was her father. He was fat and bald. No different from hundreds of sweaty-faced, bald men she had seen in her life. Elvira stared, feeling dizzy. She put the picture in her pocket and climbed in beside Aunt Carrie. All the way back, she sat and watched Aunt Carrie's hand shifting gears.

"It was nice," she said when Aunt Carrie asked about the visit. Aunt Carrie looked at her sharply and sighed. For the rest of the way home she chattered on about two patients she'd seen at the clinic. Elvira sat quietly, grateful that she didn't have to talk.

"I'm feeling a little sick," she said when they got home. "I think I'll just go and lie down."

"Your stomach upset, Elvira? Aunt Carrie asked. "You look awfully pale. Go take it easy. See if you can't get to sleep." She rested her hand on Elvira's forehead. "No fever. It's just the strain, honey. Coming up with the past like that so sudden."

Elvira nodded. She dragged herself up the stairs and fell onto her bed. Joyce's chocolate cake churned inside her. She stumbled into the bathroom and threw up. After she had rinsed off her face and taken a drink of cool water, she felt better. She went back to her room and pulled the blanket over her, feeling chilled. Just before she fell asleep, she heard Cousin Henry's voice from downstairs.

"Your own fault, subjecting that child to that! Those Judsons—just as tacky and no-account today as they ever were!"

"Hush, Henry!" Aunt Carrie said. Then the door to the kitchen shut and it was quiet. Elvira slept.

__10__

WHEN SHE woke up Saturday morning, Elvira didn't remember why she felt so strange. She sat up, blinking. Then Friday came back. Her throat tightened, and she shut her eyes. Her father was gone. The man with the tweed jacket and the pipe, who smiled at her and cared about her and was *like* her, the man who brought her roses in the hospital, who had been coming for her in his Cadillac, was gone. She was alone.

It was worse than having somebody die, finding out that somebody just never *was*, never had been, never would be. Elvira crawled back under the bedclothes and held her breath to stop her sobs. The worst thing was the feeling that she was nobody at all. Before yesterday, she had been the daughter of the man with distinguished sideburns and the warm smile. Even being surrounded by relatives who felt sorry for her, cousins who sneered at her—Elvira thought of Ellen Rose and shuddered—even that was bearable as long as she had been able to say to herself that she was better than all of them.

She wasn't better than anybody. She was a "mistake" her parents had made. And her father was never going to care what became of her, not if she lived to be a hundred and fifty. To think that she'd been waiting for that man—Joyce's brother, the "skirt-chaser"—to come and rescue her. Elvira shivered.

What on earth was she going to do? How was she going to get out of bed and get dressed? Elvira gritted her teeth. Nobody was going to guess how miserable she felt. She sat up and smoothed her hair.

She wasn't anybody's daughter. And she didn't want to be somebody's poor relation—pathetic Cousin Elvira. "Connections aren't all that great," she heard Michael's voice say. "People pulling and yanking at you." Wednesday she hadn't been ready to hear him. Now she knew what he meant. She had to be free and to live on her own. Then who her father was, whether her mother had run off and left her, would never matter. Family connections dragged you down, Elvira thought, made you apologize for yourself.

Carrie had been nice, and so had Henry. To Elvira's surprise, she felt sorrow at the thought of leaving them. But Carrie could never understand Elvira's feelings. Her life had been too different. Just accidentally being born into the same family did not make people kin, not in any real way. Elvira understood that now. She had assumed her father had to be like her, just because Laureen said so, and because he was her father.

The only one here who was like her was Michael. He was the person Elvira felt like seeing now. Remembering the way he'd talked about his mother, Elvira knew he'd understand. If she went down and had breakfast, she could slip out and run through the woods to the old house. Carrie and Henry were used to her going off by herself. Elvira got dressed.

At breakfast, she was quiet. Henry glanced at her, and rattled his newspaper at Carrie. To her relief, neither of them pressed her with questions.

Later that morning, Elvira came through the hedge and went around to the back of the house. Michael was nowhere in sight. She knocked on the door to the summer kitchen. No answer. The whole place was silent and empty in the white morning sun. Probably Michael had gone off through the woods for something. He'd told Elvira that he got canned beans and stuff at a beat-up little grocery store back in the hills where a number of black families lived. Nobody there would recognize him, or care if they did. He might be there, or he might be off hiking in the woods. Elvira's eyes widened. Suppose he had left already?

She gasped and pushed open the summer-kitchen door. His stuff was spread all over. Weak with relief, she pulled the door shut and went up to the house to wait.

Just inside the French doors, Elvira paused. She looked at the Indian print throw in the corner and thought of her story. Tears stung her eyes. She'd been taken in by fairy tales, romances, the silly stories Laureen watched on TV. Life didn't send out knights to rescue people like Elvira. All those tall men in sashes and swords she'd imagined were probably fat little tubs with hairy nostrils.

"You know what happened to the first Elvira?" she muttered. "She probably died of whooping cough. Stuffed herself on gone-by chicken and died of food poisoning." Elvira snorted.

Never again was she going to tell stories like that one, much less *believe* them.

She noticed a ragged broom on the back porch. Sweeping out was just what Elvira felt like doing. Geting rid of all the nonsense once and for all. Wednesday, she had liked the mysterious look the room had; the leaves blown here and there, the bird's nest above the door; all that had seemed right then. Today, she looked at it and said, "What a *mess!*"

Sweeping the leaves and pine needles out the front door, Elvira felt better. "Out!" she said with every sweep of the broom. "Out and good riddance!" Dust flew in a cloud around her. She almost choked, but she swept on as if she were in a race, practically bending the broomstraws double with every stroke— whissh, whissh, whissh. She stopped, panting, to catch her breath.

"Well, fire up." Michael was standing by the window, staring at her in surprise. Elvira jumped.

"I'm cleaning up," she snapped. "This place is a mess."

"Yeah," he said, puzzled.

"I was waiting for you." Elvira put the broom down. "Come in." Her voice was almost curt. "Michael," she said, trying to hold on to her newfound confidence, "when you go, I want to go with you."

"What!" He was incredulous. "You're just a kid!"

"I am not," Elvira said. "And you said yourself how people treat kids. Like they weren't human. Now you're doing it yourself."

"You've got to be crazy, Elvira." Michael pushed at his cowlick. "You can't mean this. People will be looking for you everywhere. We wouldn't have a chance."

"If you're hitchhiking, nobody is going to find us that quick. And with a girl, you'll be more likely to get picked up." She had thought of some solid arguments. "With a girl they won't think you're going to rob them or anything."

"What they'll think is that I'm carrying off some little girl— helping you run away from home." Michael shook his head. "We'd get turned in twenty miles down the road."

"Not if we explained," Elvira said. "I could say I'm your sister. We're going to stay with our married brother. His wife has just had a baby and I'm going to help out. You're going to look for a job. That makes perfectly good sense." She was pleased with the way she was putting her ability to make up stories to practical use. She leaned back, waiting for Michael's response.

"And why are we hitching? Our mother just said, 'Take little Elvira, Sonny, and hitch across the country. Save a little bread.' They're going to believe that, too?" He shook his head.

"We can think of something to explain that," Elvira said. "It won't be that hard."

"Forget it, Elvira. You aren't coming."

"Listen, Michael," Elvira said, turning white, "I am. You get that. I am. Or else just say good-bye to this place and living here by yourself and all. Because I'll tell. Just where you are." She hated herself for saying that, but she had no choice.

"You wouldn't do that!" Michael stared at her.

"Oh yes I would!" Elvira cringed against the wall. She thought he might jump on her, strangle her or something. "And keep away from me!"

"Oh, Jesus, shut up." Michael said. "I'm not going to hurt you." He drew patterns on the floor with one finger. "Listen. Let's work out some kind of deal for now."

"What kind of deal?" Elvira asked, narrowing her eyes. "You aren't thinking to run out on me?"

"When I say something," Michael said, "I mean it. Not like some people."

Elvira turned red. "If I could help it, I wouldn't do this, Michael. If things weren't impossible." She picked at the hem of the throw. "I can't stand to stay here anymore."

Michael sighed. "Yeah. I guessed something bad was happening when I saw you. You really look wiped out. What is it? You still looking for your father?"

"No," Elvira said. "I'm not. What I'm doing is just what you said. Getting away from being tied down to other people. I'm going to be free and live by myself."

"You might have trouble, Elvira," Michael said. "Passing for old enough. You might get stuck in a foster home or something."

"I'd rather," she said. "At least they couldn't claim to be kin, pushing at me to be like them. And they'd just get paid for taking care of me, wouldn't they? I wouldn't have to be grateful or anything."

"Well, if you know what you're getting into," Michael said, "we can talk it over, at least. In some ways, it would be good." He paused. "I get lonesome, by myself all the time." He looked away. "I'm not saying I don't."

"I appreciated your helping me, Michael," Elvira said quietly. "I just thought I would like to go with you, that's all." Her voice quavered slightly. "I kind of felt like you were the only person around here I could feel OK with."

Michael turned pink. "I didn't mean to yell at you, Elvira. You've been all right. Bringing me sandwiches and stuff, not

99

telling I'm here. What I mean about a deal is, let's work out a plan. Maybe for next week. I figure to be all set by Tuesday or Wednesday. By then, we'll have decided something, one way or the other."

"You mean it?" Elvira gasped. She wouldn't have told on him, no matter what, but she was amazed that he'd agreed so quickly. "I just have to get on my own, that's all," she said. "Like you. You can understand that."

"Sure. As long as you know what's in front of you. You can't come into this and half a mile down the road start crying your eyes out for your mamma or anything like that."

"Good luck on crying for *Laureen!* She ran off and left me, for God's sake!" She was feeling tougher every minute. "I'll go to Chicago," she said, plucking a broomstraw and sticking the clean end in her mouth. "By then Laureen will be back or close to it. If she doesn't want me with her and Duane, swell. She can help me find a place of my own." She was feeling better and better. "They can just eat my dust."

Michael laughed. "You're a tough kid, Elvira. You're starting to make a lot of sense. Let's just tell everybody to shove it, and be on our way."

Elvira nodded, her eyes bright. She and Michael looked at each other, suddenly shy. "I've got to get back soon," Elvira stammered. "I promised to be back for lunch."

Michael got to his feet hastily. "I'll walk partway with you," he said. As they walked through the French doors, he took her hand. They crossed the field, holding hands.

11

ENOUGH OF this moping around here, young lady," Aunt Carrie said to Elvira Sunday morning. "I don't care what you say, I think you need company, a little cheering up." She wiped the table with a damp cloth. "I'm having people over. Get your mind off things."

"Who's coming?" Cousin Henry asked, filling his pipe.

"Louise and Jimmy and Ellen Rose. I asked them for an afternoon dinner, so we'll need to bustle around, Elvira, to get everything ready."

"I don't feel all that great," Elvira said. "I think I might be catching the flu or something. Probably I should stay upstairs while they are here. You wouldn't want Ellen Rose catching anything."

Aunt Carrie felt her forehead. "No fever. I think you'll be all right. Just get busy for a while. The best medicine for anybody." She hung the cloth back on the rack over the sink. "Maybe you could snap the beans while I get the roast going." Elvira sighed and pulled the stool up to the sink.

Ellen Rose came swinging across the porch behind her mother. Her hair was swept up in two ponytails and her fingernails were painted opal.

"Look at this!" Cousin Louise exclaimed to Aunt Carrie. "Doesn't she look like some ghoul—ready for Halloween? Says she got it out of *Seventeen* magazine. Never in all my life." She shook her head and smiled indulgently at Ellen Rose. "I'm sure you'd never go in for anything as silly as that, Elvira!"

Elvira felt uncomfortable. She didn't want to defend Ellen Rose, but she didn't want to side with the old people, either. Kissing up to adults was what Ellen Rose always did. "I think it looks OK," Elvira said. "Kind of like pearls."

"See there. That's what the magazine said," Ellen Rose exclaimed. She looked at Elvira gratefully. " 'A pearly opalescent look for the summer months'!"

"Well," her mother said, "at least it comes off. You aren't tattooing yourself or anything—yet." She looked at Aunt Carrie and they both laughed. They moved toward the kitchen, to put Cousin Louise's potato salad in the refrigerator.

Ellen Rose looked at Elvira and raised her eyebrows. For a second they almost smiled at each other. Then Elvira caught herself and looked away.

"You two girls entertain yourselves for a while," Aunt Carrie called out. "Louise and I have everything under control in here."

"What do you want to do?" Elvira asked guardedly.

"You are the one that lives here," Ellen Rose drawled. "You're the hostess."

Elvira looked at Ellen Rose. She was dressed fit to kill. "I remember how you said you loved walking in the woods out back. Wading in the mud, making dams, all that. Let's go and take a hike before dinner."

Ellen Rose swallowed. "Let's just go upstairs and sit around your room, Elvira," she said. "Look at your things. It's kind of hot and buggy for going outside."

Elvira smiled and started up the stairs. As she stretched her hand onto the banister knob, she felt Ellen Rose looking at her fingernails. They were bitten to the quick. Elvira snatched her hand away.

"We could polish your nails for you, just like mine," Ellen Rose suggested sweetly. "Then we'd match."

"Thank you," Elvira said as offhandedly as she could. "I don't think I want to take the time today." She swept up the stairs, Ellen Rose behind her.

"Well, it's up to you," Ellen Rose said. "I just like to be friendly, is all. Since we *are* cousins." She came in and plopped down on Elvira's bed.

"Sure," Elvira said. "I know how friendly you want to be. I caught on to that *last* Sunday. The very first day I got here."

"What on earth are you talking about?" Ellen Rose's eyes opened wide.

"The way you shoved that door back at me the first day I came, for one thing." Elvira glared at her.

Ellen Rose turned pink. "I think you've lost your mind. I never shoved any door at you."

103

Liar, thought Elvira. She got up stiffly. "Well, you wanted to see my things. They are in there. Look all you want to." She pulled two bureau drawers open, turned her back on Ellen Rose and walked over to the window. She looked toward the woods and tried to think about Michael.

"I hear you've been trying to find your daddy. Hoping he'll come and take you back to the city to live? Like you said he might?"

Elvira clutched the folds of the curtain and clenched her teeth. She should never have said anything to Ellen Rose about her dreams. Now there was nothing she could do. "Just leave my father and what I plan to do alone!" she hissed. "It's none of your business!"

"Well, *excuse me,* I'm sure," Ellen Rose said.

Elvira wheeled around, but she couldn't speak. Just saying the words *my father* had done it. She held her breath, she tried to pretend she was sneezing, but nothing worked. Elvira started sobbing. She leaned back into the curtains, her shoulders heaving. She gasped and tears streamed down her face.

Ellen Rose stared at her in astonishment. "Elvira," she said, "what's the matter?"

"What do you care?" Elvira gasped out. "You hypocrite. Asking me what's the matter." She bit her lip until it bled, but she couldn't stop her heaving sobs.

Ellen Rose's green eyes were wide. For a long time she didn't say anything. Then she turned and looked out the window, sniffling once herself. "I didn't know you felt bad," she said. "How was I supposed to know that?"

"How did you think I felt?" Elvira managed to say. "What

104

could you possibly think a person dumped off in the woods to live with strangers was going to feel?"

"Well, I don't know," Ellen Rose said with tears in her eyes, "that you have been exactly great to me, either. Coming here, taking my place, expecting me to move over. Next fall you'll be doing the same thing in school. I won't have a friend left!"

Elvira stared. "What are you talking about? How could I do all that?"

"Just by walking in the door, that's how," Ellen Rose snapped. "*You* know everybody is dying to meet you already. *You* know that you can just sashay in, the big-city girl, and take over everything."

Elvira was astonished. She hadn't thought for one minute that Ellen Rose could be jealous of her.

"And you haven't been all that nice to me, either," Ellen Rose continued. "I practically fainted when you told Mamma my nail polish looked all right. That's the first barely decent thing you've said to me all week." She sniffled and wiped her nose with a tissue from Elvira's dresser. "Everybody at school is going to want to be your friend. You'll be the most popular person in our class. Nobody is going to notice me anymore. How do you think I like knowing that?"

"Why would people want to know me?"

"Because you are new, and lived in Chicago. And you ought to have seen how Mamma and all those ladies clustered around after church, clucking on about how *lovely* you are." She glared at Elvira.

"I thought everybody was saying how pathetic I am. How my own mother won't even take care of me."

105

"Shoot, everybody remembers Laureen." Ellen Rose looked embarrassed. "I don't mean there's anything wrong with your mother, but everybody knows she was never too dependable. At least that's what my mother says. But she says you are a real credit to her. 'Laureen must have had more going for her than we noticed, Jimmy,' Mamma said, 'to bring up a girl like that.' "

"Really?" Elvira was flustered. None of this fit what she had been thinking. "Laureen isn't so bad," she found herself saying. "Having to manage by herself so long. Working crummy jobs and all."

"I didn't mean she was," Ellen Rose said. "But it doesn't make any difference about you anyway. My dad thinks you'll be a lot of help to Aunt Carrie."

"Not a burden on her?" Elvira couldn't resist, even though she was starting to feel friendlier to Ellen Rose.

Ellen Rose flushed beet-red. "I should never have said that, but I was so jealous. I just about turn green when I think of you having such a romantic life. First off in the big city for years, and then coming to live in this old house with its tragic past and all."

"This house? What's romantic or tragic about this house?"

Ellen Rose gasped. "You mean you never heard about the shooting? Laureen never told you about it?"

"No," Elvira said. "What are you talking about?"

"Aunt Carrie's parents, for heaven's sake. You must have heard!" Ellen Rose sat down on the bed. "The whole family knows about it."

"I don't. Tell me."

"It happened when Aunt Carrie was eight or nine years old," Ellen Rose said.

"She did tell me there was an accident," Elvira said.

"Well, I guess that's what it was, more or less. Anyway, Aunt Carrie's father was sort of strange—moody, hard to get along with. Henry—downstairs, Cousin Henry—he's just a distant cousin. You know, everybody around here is kin."

"Yes, yes," Elvira said. "Tell me what happened."

"Well, Cousin Henry was always a family friend. He saw how things were, and he tried to help out. Help Aunt Carrie's mother and all. He felt sorry for her, and the children, too."

"Her father was that bad?"

"Yeah, he was really strange, and he drank a lot, I guess. Anyway, one day it all just exploded." Ellen Rose gazed dramatically out the window, as if overcome by what she was about to tell. "This little place in the woods became the scene of a tragedy that left everybody stunned for miles around. My mamma's eyes still fill with tears when she tells about it. I can't believe Laureen didn't mention it." She turned to look at Elvira.

This was the old Ellen Rose. "What happened, Ellen Rose?" Elvira snapped. "For heaven's sake, get to the point."

"It took place downstairs," Ellen Rose drawled, rolling her eyes toward the ceiling. "In the very room where we will soon be sitting down to eat Sunday dinner."

"The shooting?" Elvira asked. "*Who* shot them?"

"Aunt Carrie's father, in his deranged state, suddenly snatched up the gun," Ellen Rose finally said. "He shot his wife, Isabelle, Cousin Henry and himself. Everybody but Cousin Henry, fatally." She paused to let the impact of this register on Elvira. "Isabelle was only in her twenties. They say she was really beautiful, that everyone was just devoted to her. It put the whole family into a state of shock. You can imagine."

"What about Aunt Carrie? Where was she?"

"In the beginning, when Buford first started shooting, she was in the room. But then she grabbed her baby sister and ran out with her. Mamma says that's undoubtedly what saved those two babies, Carrie's remarkable presence of mind at the time. She was only eight or nine—imagine! Well, she ran out and crouched down on the stairs, behind the banisters. That's the picture that comes into my head, clear as day, every time I walk up those steps," Ellen Rose confided. "I see Aunt Carrie, crunched down and big-eyed, a little girl afraid for her life."

"How incredible!" Elvira gasped. "I can't believe it!"

Ellen Rose nodded. "I've often thought that if a famous novelist heard that story, this little house would become a famous place. And there's more to it, too. Afterward, Cousin Henry, crippled as he was, insisted on taking responsibility for the girls; he devoted his life to raising them."

"Cousin Henry?"

"Yes, gave up his life to Carrie and Elizabeth. Crippled as he was, there was many a lady would have been willing to marry him, Mamma says. According to her, he was the best-looking young man in Charlottesville!"

"Cousin Henry?" Elvira thought of the crotchety figure in the wheelchair, pulling at his afghan with knotted fingers. "Cousin Henry was that good-looking?"

"And rich, too. Or at least he had an independent income—enough to live on all his life and take care of the girls and all." Ellen Rose smoothed out the spread. "Mamma says Aunt Carrie never got over the shock completely, and that's why she's never married or anything. People say she is so kind and takes care of everybody because she suffered so much herself. A shock like that changes a person's psychology, makes them a little different. Don't you feel that about Aunt Carrie? That she's a person set apart somehow?"

"Set apart." The phrase made Elvira shiver a little. Aunt Carrie, "set apart" by living through tragedy at such a young age. Bravely going on, but always at a little distance from other people, because a part of her was always back in the past, seeing her lovely mother shot dead before her eyes.

At dinner, Elvira stole little glances at Aunt Carrie. The squared set to her shoulders, the way her hair was streaked with gray and pulled back so severely, even the lines at the corners of her mouth, all said something different to Elvira now. For the first time, she felt a real connection to her aunt. There is a person who has suffered, Elvira thought. A person who has a secret life inside her. "Delicious roast, Aunt Carrie," she said aloud.

"You're looking better, Elvira," Aunt Carrie said. "I knew a little company was the thing." She smiled in a pleased way.

12

*A*FTER THE others had left, Elvira and Aunt Carrie did the dishes. Cousin Henry sat at the table smoking his pipe and keeping them company. Knowing what she did about their past, Elvira felt as if Aunt Carrie and Cousin Henry were new people, different entirely from the ordinary pair she had known before. She felt a gentle sadness, a pleasant feeling that blended with the quiet of the house and the soft light of evening. The whirring hum of insects that always came with twilight had begun. Soon lightning bugs would be blinking on and off, floating above the grass. "I like bug noises," she said dreamily to Uncle Henry.

"I always have myself," he agreed. "Like a little orchestra out there, playing in the grass."

"It would take you two"—Aunt Carrie smiled indulgently at them—"to listen to a bunch of locusts rubbing their legs together and hear violins. What a pair of starry-eyed romantics!"

"Nothing wrong with that," Cousin Henry said. "Is there, Elvira?" He smiled. "As long as we have somebody like Carrie around to keep us on the track, rub our noses in the grim realities."

Aunt Carrie sniffed. "Just as long as you keep in mind that bugs are bugs," she said, "whatever they sound like. And they do sound pretty," she admitted with a smile, after a minute's pause. "I never said they didn't." She reached over to the stove for the roasting pan. Midway, she stopped and turned. "Elvira! I was supposed to tell you something." She looked concerned. "Before he left, Jimmy asked me to tell you to stay close to the house for a week or so. No wandering in the woods for a while."

"Why not?" Henry asked. "What's going on?"

"He's after somebody. Has reason to think someone's hanging around the old Matthews place."

"That's my fault," Cousin Henry exclaimed. "You tried to tell me we shouldn't let Elvira wander off in the woods. I should have listened. Times have changed—there's no telling who might be back there!" He put down his pipe, frowning.

"Now, calm down," Aunt Carrie said. "I knew you'd get all flustered. That's why I waited to bring it up. Jimmy didn't think it was anything dangerous. Just that it would be wise to take a few precautions until they find out who's over there." She picked up the pan and started scraping it.

"Do they have any idea who the person is?" Elvira asked.

"Not that Jimmy mentioned. They don't like to speculate on that sort of thing anyway, until they're sure. So Jimmy wouldn't have said." Carrie dumped the grease into a can by the sink and filled the roaster with soapy water to soak. She dried her hands on her apron. "He just spoke to me, us being the only house around and Elvira wandering around the woods and all. You haven't seen anything suspicious, have you, Elvira?"

"Of course she hasn't!" Cousin Henry snapped. "You don't think Elvira would keep anything like that to herself, do you?"

Elvira shook her head. Her heart was thumping and she was a little out of breath.

"No need to scare yourself, honey," Aunt Carrie said. "I doubt you were ever in any danger, and you certainly won't be now. Just stay out of the woods until Jimmy picks them up." She handed Elvira a dry towel. The two of them finished drying the silver. Cousin Henry rolled himself into the living room and turned on the TV.

"He never watches TV unless he needs to calm his nerves," Aunt Carrie whispered to Elvira. "Gets his mind off things. That man dotes on you, has ever since you came."

Elvira blushed. She was touched by the way Henry had gotten so upset. Nobody had ever been that worried about her. "He's awfully nice," she said.

"Honey," Carrie said, "you're looking peaked again—pale as a sheet. Probably too much of a good thing, all this company. Why don't you go on up and rest?"

As soon as they finished in the kitchen, Elvira took Aunt Carrie's advice and trudged up the stairs to her room. Her hands were ice-cold. Michael couldn't be dragged back to his family by the sheriff—he'd never stand up straight again.

At three A.M., Elvira crept out of the house. "You could do this blindfolded, Elvira," she muttered. "Don't be a coward." Familiar as it was, the path was bumpier in the dark; she caught her clothes on vines and had to pull loose twice. Crossing the creek, she slipped and stepped into the icy water up to her ankle. By the time she came out of the woods, she was panting.

"Michael! Michael!" She thumped on the door to the summer kitchen.

"Elvira?" The door opened a crack. "What?"

"Get out, Michael! They're after you. The sheriff is coming. They know somebody is here."

He blinked at her. Then he pulled the door open all the way to let her in. "OK. I'll be ready in a second. Are they coming now?"

"No. But they're planning to."

He turned on a flashlight and grabbed a backpack off a hook on the wall. "I've kept this ready to go—food, sleeping bag, everything," he said. "And I sleep in my clothes." He beamed the light around, locating his shoes. He sat on the floor and tied them, rolled up his sleeping bag, tied it to the backpack and held the door for Elvira. "Let's go," he said. "The faster I'm out of here, the better."

"Where will you go?"

"Across the mountain." Michael pointed toward the woods in back of the cemetery. "I'll walk for a couple of days, camping. That will get me through to the main road west—a long ways from here." He put his arms through the straps and bounced the pack, settling it. "Right now, though, I'll just go back a ways into the woods and wait for it to get lighter. No use getting lost before I get started." Michael tried to laugh, but his voice squeaked. They trotted off toward the woods.

"We could sit here," Michael said a little later, "and wait for

113

it to get light." He slipped his pack off, and they sat down against a pine tree. "Elvira, I guess you saved my skin, coming out this way."

He looked around for a stick to chew. His hands trembled slightly as he peeled a twig. "Michael," Elvira said, "why don't you go back home? Just to see how it would work out? Things might be different now."

He grimaced. "No way. I've had it." He stuck the twig between his teeth. "You aren't coming?" Elvira shook her head and looked away. "You're right," he said quickly. "You're too young. Would slow me down." He pulled on the strap to his pack.

Elvira felt rotten. "Couldn't you work out something here, Michael?" she said in a small voice. "I guess I ought to stay after all. Aunt Carrie and Cousin Henry are my family, after all."

"Found out they weren't as bad as you thought, huh?"

"They've had a sad life," Elvira said. "Ellen Rose was telling me. I think they need me here."

"She told you about the shooting?"

"You know about that?"

"I know more than Ellen Rose does. More than anybody else except for Carrie and Henry. You remember I told you I heard them talking?"

"That day you were working? What did they say?"

"Well, she was saying what you would expect—that he'd taken care of her when she needed somebody, and now his back was getting worse, and he was going to have to use the chair for getting around all the time. She was trying to persuade him to come and stay with her."

"Yes. I heard that's how it was."

114

"Yeah, but he said it wasn't that simple. He said he took care of her and her sister, not just to be nice, the way everybody thought, but because it was his fault—what happened."

"But he got crippled himself, trying to stop Aunt Carrie's father. Ellen Rose said Aunt Carrie's father was crazy."

"Yeah, but he was crazy for a reason. Your Uncle Buford was always a hard man to get along with, your Cousin Henry said. And he got weirder, and was drinking and all. At first your Cousin Henry was trying to help out because he was an old family friend."

"At first?"

"Then he fell in love with Isabelle, your Aunt Carrie's mother," Michael said. "I guess they were both in love and they didn't know what to do. People didn't get divorced back then, and they felt bad about her husband and there were the children and all."

"Oh, how awful," Elvira said, seeing what was coming.

"Yeah, he said he should have left—your Cousin Henry kept saying that over and over. 'Carrie, I should have had the strength to go,' he said three or four times. But he didn't. And Buford found out, and that's when he started shooting at everybody. 'I was the one he should have killed, and I was the only one he missed,' your Cousin Henry said."

Elvira sat, stunned. For a second, she caught herself thinking how Ellen Rose's mouth would drop open if she ever heard this story. But she could never tell anyone. "Michael," she said, "it was nice of you to keep quiet about it."

"Henry felt awful. He'd never wanted anybody to know. They were both crying, Elvira. Old as they were. Crying. And she said it was OK. Said she'd sort of known anyway. 'We do the

115

best we can, Henry,' she said—I still hear her saying that—'we do the best we can.' Then I knocked over a glass, and they found out I was there. I felt rotten. Henry was just humiliated, because I'd heard him crying and all." Michael looked at the ground.

Cousin Henry, stiff as a soldier in his chair, was a lot like Michael, Elvira suddenly realized. Proud.

It was getting noticeably lighter. Michael started picking up his pack. "Michael, *can't* you stay?" Elvira pleaded. Tears were stinging the back of her nose.

He shook his head. "Never."

"Maybe I *will* come," she burst out. "I want to go and I want to stay."

"Coming would be stupid. I told you that from the first." He adjusted the straps. "I better not wait any longer. I should get going. Thanks, Elvira." He turned toward her awkwardly and reached out as if he were planning to shake hands. Then he leaned toward her and caught her shoulders. He kissed her on the lips. "Good-bye, ghost girl," he said, trying to laugh. "I'll write you—a code or something so nobody will know. I'll do great.. Don't worry." He headed off into the woods.

Elvira stared at the bushes long after they had closed behind Michael. No boy had ever kissed her before. She strained to hear his footsteps disappearing. Then she turned and started back slowly, coming out of the woods behind the cemetery at the deserted house. Her thoughts were on Michael, picturing him striding through the wilderness behind her, brave and alone. When she looked up and caught sight of the house looming ahead of her at the end of the garden, she was startled. The sun

116

was just behind it; here and there, a window glowed bright pink. Birds were starting to call. Elvira held her breath. Morning mist, ground fog from the dew, made the house float as if it were in the clouds. It looked like part of the sky with the lavender and pink and gold of the sunrise behind it. Columns of mist, almost like figures, floated across the porch. It was a vision.

When the rose and purple sky turned to familiar blue, Elvira felt as if she had been released from a spell. She ran inside the house and got her Indian throw. No need to let Cousin Jimmy find it. Then she ran across the field to the woods. Still dazed by what she had seen, Elvira didn't look back once.

At Carrie's, she crept in the back door and tiptoed up to her room. As she lay down, she smelled the delicate scent of mimosa from the tree by her window. With it, pink and golden like a mimosa flower, came the vision of the house in the woods. She dozed off. When she woke up, it was full morning.

Elvira had saved the boy she loved. The thought made her eyes shine. Brushing her hair, Elvira realized she could let Ellen Rose know *a little* about Michael. Not who he was, for sure, but that there was *somebody,* a secret boy she had once loved and helped to escape. Tall and blond.

Elvira fastened her hair with a barrette. It was time to go downstairs. Suddenly she wanted to sit at the table and eat eggs with Cousin Henry and Aunt Carrie. Like them, she had been through a tragedy, and like them, she had secrets from the world.

"Little Cousin Elvira, fresh as a flower." Cousin Henry beamed at her.

Elvira went over and kissed him. "Good morning," she said.

117

"Look, Ellie." Aunt Carrie came in from the porch, holding three or four letters. "From Laureen." She handed Elvira a postcard.

Sure enough, it was a picture of a big set of gates to a southern mansion. "Graceland, former home of Elvis Presley."

"I knew that's where they'd be going," Elvira said, flipping the card over. "Laureen always wanted to see it."

"Well, she always was the romantic type," Aunt Carrie said, reaching into the refrigerator for the eggs.

"Yeah," Elvira said absently, reading Laureen's breathless message on the back. "And it's good that things are finally working out for her."